Live Borders

3 4144 0103 3124 3

C COLDSTREAM
TEL:883804
INNERLEITH
TEL:83078

D0715744

WITHDRAWN

SPECIAL MESSAGE TO READERS

THE ULVERSCROFT FOUNDATION
(registered UK charity number 264873)

was established in 1972 to provide funds for research, diagnosis and treatment of eye diseases. Examples of major projects funded by the Ulverscroft Foundation are:-

- The Children's Eye Unit at Moorfields Eye Hospital, London
- The Ulverscroft Children's Eye Unit at Great Ormond Street Hospital for Sick Children
- Funding research into eye diseases and treatment at the Department of Ophthalmology, University of Leicester
- The Ulverscroft Vision Research Group, Institute of Child Health
- Twin operating theatres at the Western Ophthalmic Hospital, London
- The Chair of Ophthalmology at the Royal Australian College of Ophthalmologists

You can help further the work of the Foundation by making a donation or leaving a legacy. Every contribution is gratefully received. If you would like to help support the Foundation or require further information, please contact:

THE ULVERSCROFT FOUNDATION
The Green, Bradgate Road, Anstey
Leicester LE7 7FU, England
Tel: (0116) 236 4325
website: www.foundation.ulverscroft.com

THE MISSING MAN

Writer Cindy Carter accepts a routine assignment from her editor: fly to Athens, write some articles, and fit in an interview with an elderly professor who insists he's got something important to say. But what occurs is anything but routine. Her case is accidentally switched with that of another passenger containing one hundred thousand dollars in cash. When the professor is killed in an explosion, Cindy becomes embroiled in an assassination plot involving a Russian terrorist, and must assist NATO agents in capturing the missing man.

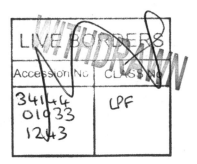

LIVE BORDERS
WITHDRAWN

Accession No	Class No
34144 01033 1243	LPF

Books by V. J. Banis
in the Linford Mystery Library:

THE WOLVES OF CRAYWOOD
THE GLASS PAINTING
WHITE JADE
DARKWATER
I AM ISABELLA
THE GLASS HOUSE
MOON GARDEN
THE SECOND HOUSE
ROSE POINT
THE DEVIL'S DANCE
SHADOWS
HOUSE OF FOOLS
FIVE GREEN MEN
THE SCENT OF HEATHER
THE BISHOP'S PALACE
BLOOD MOON
FIRE ON THE MOON
FATAL FLOWERS
THE LION'S GATE
TILL THE DAY I DIE
THE MYSTERY OF BLOODSTONE
PRISONER OF KELSEY HOUSE
THE MISTRESS OF EVIL
GHOST LAKE
MYSTERY OF THE RUBY
HAUNTED HELEN

V. J. BANIS

THE
MISSING
MAN

Complete and Unabridged

LINFORD
Leicester

First published in Great Britain

First Linford Edition
published 2019

Copyright © 2018 by V. J. Banis
All rights reserved

A catalogue record for this book is available
from the British Library.

ISBN 978–1–4448–4111–4

Published by
F. A. Thorpe (Publishing)
Anstey, Leicestershire

Set by Words & Graphics Ltd.
Anstey, Leicestershire
Printed and bound in Great Britain by
T. J. International Ltd., Padstow, Cornwall

This book is printed on acid-free paper

1

Athens, Greece, 1956

How did people do it? Cindy Carter wondered. It was not the first time she had asked herself that question, either? How on earth did they sleep more or less sitting up in an airplane, and apparently sleep quite well? She personally had never managed to master the art of sleeping on a plane, period. What she experienced were nothing more than cat naps that pretended to be slumber but were filled with jumps and starts every time the plane's engines changed pitch, which they seemed to do incessantly.

But other people could sleep just fine like that, it seemed. They could fly all the way from New York City and still manage to arrive in Athens, Greece, almost a full day later looking like they had just stepped out of a beauty salon.

She herself had done all the prescribed

steps, the things that magazine articles told you were the way to manage on an airplane. (As a writer for a magazine herself, she was a big believer in what magazines recommended she do.) She had donned a sleep mask precisely three hours into the flight and had splashed cold water on her face upon waking from what had been, the mask notwithstanding, no more than a half-sleep. She had even, in that tiny restroom and while the plane jerked and bounced around, managed to put on a new coating of makeup in the morning, which, according to the magazines, was supposed to make her feel ready to face a new world, though they never mentioned what world that was. Presumably they did not mean the one in which she actually lived.

And for all her efforts, she had not needed to look into the mirror in that diminutive restroom to know that she looked like she had just spent the night flying over the Atlantic and half a day more flying over Europe as well. She looked just the way she always looked after a long flight, and that was like she had been up all night.

Whereas the young lady who had been in the row just ahead of her for the whole flight and was now striding purposefully through the busy air terminal in Athens looked like she might just have stepped from the pages of a fashion magazine. Her eyes and lips were perfectly painted (when had she slipped into the restroom, Cindy wondered? She had not seen her go. Or had she somehow wrought this miracle of make-up in her seat? That was too incredible even to contemplate, surely.) Not to mention that every hair was where some clever stylist back in Manhattan had meant it to be, and not a one astray. Her chic Chanel suit in which she had spent the entire flight showed no evidence of the wear and tear — nary a wrinkle nor untoward crease to be seen. She carried a tiny purse (too tiny to be practical, one would think) in one hand and a small overnight case in the other. A case not unlike my own, Cindy found herself thinking, even the same off-white color, and which was almost certainly the only thing the two of them had in common.

For a fleeting moment, approaching the customs inspectors in their little cubicles, Cindy wished their bureaucratic wrath would somehow descend upon her plane mate. Which thought she quickly dismissed as petty and unworthy. It was hardly the woman's fault if she was by nature elegant and chic, as Cindy knew perfectly well she was not.

Then, her turn in the customs line came up, and she was too busy answering questions to think about Miss Perfection, as she had dubbed her.

No, I'm not smuggling anything, was what she wanted to say, and be done with the beating around the bush, but she smiled and said all the proper things you were supposed to say during such an interview: Yes, she was here on business (which she had every hope could be combined with a little pleasure as well, but she did not tell the customs inspector that, which would almost certainly have led to more questions). What kind of business, he wanted to know? I am a writer, she explained in her most patient voice, telling herself not to fidget. A writer? Yes, she informed him, for the magazine, Columbine, a New York City magazine but with a branch here in Athens also.

No, she was not intending to remain in Athens indefinitely: she was here only for two weeks, and then straight home. Unless, of course, she could think of some way to convince old man Baker, her boss back in New York, that she needed, for some reason she had not yet managed to dream up, a little side trip, time for nothing but relaxing and pampering herself. A trip to, say, Paris, where she could certainly manage to relax and pamper herself. But there was no point in mentioning that to the funny little man in the rumpled uniform who was interrogating her and who looked as though he little cared what anyone's dreams might be, hers least of all.

In any case, she knew, if her interrogator did not, that her boss was not an easy man to convince, not when it came to spending company money for side trips to dream cities.

Which meant that if she was to go to

Paris, she would have to pay her own way. Which meant as well that Paris would certainly have to remain a dream. Magazine writers, even staff writers, did not make that kind of money, not Paris money. Even with the little bonus he had added to her salary, to do that interview for him while she was here, she still could not afford it. Paris must remain what it had ever been: a dream. And dreams were often expensive. Prohibitively expensive.

'He's just a harmless old college professor,' Mr. Baker had explained, in asking her if she would mind terribly doing that interview as a favor for him. 'I knew him from my long ago student days in Athens. I studied philosophy under him. And now the man insists he has got something important to say and he is sure I would want to hear it.'

'But you don't,' she had suggested, tilting one eyebrow.

'Frankly, I doubt it amounts to a hill of beans, one way or another,' Baker had said. 'Look, at worst it won't take up more than an hour or so of your time. More than likely not even that. You will probably decide in your first fifteen minutes that the man is nothing but a crackpot. That's fine. All I ask is that you be an angel and treat him gently, will you? The old boy was awfully kind to me in those student days. And I did manage to learn a smattering of Plato and Aristotle. For which I owe him at least a semblance of attention, I think.'

Well, Mr. Baker was paying her generously enough for the added work, which from what he had told her would probably be hardly any work at all, and which she must somehow manage to squeeze in among her pieces on Athens, the birthplace of democracy. She had already settled on that for the tagline; it was not very original, true, but she thought it worked. And Columbine was not known for breaking new ground.

She would decide over her first few days here on the specific locations she wanted to write about: the Acropolis, of course, and the royal palace and those guards in their funny uniforms with the long leggings and the pom-poms on their boots. And maybe, if it could be easily arranged, a trip to Delphi. Lots of beautiful ruins there, and staggering vistas; not to mention that theater up in the hills. Yes, she thought, she must somehow definitely work in Delphi.

She had plenty of time, too, to decide on the subjects, the slants, if you wanted to think of them that way, for her essays, and Jan Peterson, who was scheduled to follow her to Greece three days later, would do the requisite photographs for each location.

She had worked with Jan before multiple times, so she knew up front that he did first rate work. He was quite possibly the best photographer in the magazine business, which meant that she would have to be at the top of her own form to measure up; but, really, how hard could a series of travel pieces on Athens be?

If her memory of the city from a trip nearly a decade earlier was even half accurate, the pieces would pretty much write themselves. You had only to look around you in Athens, really only to breathe the air, to get the sense of democracy's birth. It was practically written on the wind. People here just inhaled it.

By this time the man in the rumpled uniform had finished with her interrogation, apparently satisfied that she was neither a smuggler nor an international jewel thief. She hoisted her purse over her shoulder, wondering as she made her way past his cubicle if they actually had international jewels in Athens? Well, yes, she thought, if not jewels, exactly, there was no shortage of treasures in those museums. Although how one 'stole' an old Greek statue was a little hard to imagine. It certainly was not something you could carry home in your purse, a thought which made her giggle aloud, causing a passing stranger to look at her nervously and hurry past.

A porter was waiting at the end of the corridor with one of those baggage trolleys, already half loaded with piled up luggage. She glanced at the woman waiting impatiently beside him. Yes, just as she had thought at first look: the waiting woman was Miss Perfection from her flight, still looking entirely unruffled and all too eager to be on her way.

Miss Perfection chose that moment to give the porter an impatient glance and a quick huff, which he pretended to neither see nor hear. After all, from his point of view, a half-filled trolley meant half the tips. Still, he clearly did not want to drag things out either, to where the other woman cut her tip in half. He caught Cindy's eye as she emerged from the customs line and made a hand gesture to get her attention.

'Can I fetch your bags for you, Kyria?' he asked.

'Yes, of course,' She answered with a quick smile. 'Those two there, the brown leather ones, and the overnighter, please.' She pointed to be sure he understood. People here mostly spoke good English, but in her experience things could also easily get confused.

'The young lady is going into the city, yes? So she will be wanting a taxi also, perhaps?' he asked, fetching the bags she had indicated and smiling broadly.

'Indeed, she will. I will.' Probably, she

thought, there was a bus, and that would certainly be cheaper than a taxi, but for all practical purposes she had been up a night and a day. This was not the time to be worrying herself overmuch about money. If the accounting office balked over the vouchers for her expenses, then she would just eat the taxi fare herself, out of that interview bonus, and be done with it. Just now, she was too tired to care.

She watched the man sling her bags easily up atop the stack on the trolley. They had just turned as a group to make their way in a neat little formation toward the exit, Miss Perfection in the lead, the porter tugging at the now heavily laden trolley and puffing noisily to show how hard he was working for his tips, and Cindy trailing after them, when something extraordinary happened.

Miss Perfection fainted.

2

Mike Dillon cut across two lanes of fast moving traffic and parked his little sports car at the curb outside the air terminal. He paused getting out of his car to glance at his watch. Yes, he was actually a little late, but hopefully that only meant Miss Carter would already have made it through the customs line and would be ready to leave for the city.

Miss Carter. He had only to think about her and he started seething anew. He paused for a moment outside the door to the terminal to get himself together. After all, old man Baker had apparently chosen her himself for this job, which meant she must have some pull in the New York office. The last thing he needed, or wanted to do was get off on the wrong foot with one of the owner's pet writers.

Was she a pet, he wondered cattily? Or perhaps something even more intimate than that? True, Baker was pushing seventy if he was a day, but he would not by a long shot be the first old codger to fall for a beautiful young woman. And Mike was willing to bet, Cindy Carter would prove to be beautiful indeed. Yes, he had met her once before, some years back, on a trip to New York, but apparently she had not made much of an impression, since he remembered her not at all.

Or had not, in any event, until he pushed his way through the terminal doors and saw her waiting just a few feet away, discussing luggage with a porter. The moment he saw her, it all came back. And, yes, he had been right, she was definitely a looker. He wondered, in fact, how on earth he had managed to forget her.

Well, give the guy credit, he thought wryly, Old man Baker had taste, in any case.

*　*　*

At least, it seemed to Cindy that Miss Perfection had fainted. One moment she was striding purposefully forward, in front of the porter and his trolley, her heels tapping out a hasty staccato on the hard tile of the terminal floor. And the next moment, she had stopped dead still and, in the same instant, sunk to the tile with a deep sigh. Her smart little purse left her hands and flew open as she fell, sending its contents willy-nilly across the floor.

Cindy looked around, wondering what on earth might have caused her to faint, but so far as she could see, there was nothing amiss. A policeman in full uniform had just come in from the street outside, brushing some dust off his sleeve. Which meant she probably would not need the worn but still serviceable slicker she carried over one arm. She ought to have remembered: rain was apparently illegal in Greece: it seemed never to happen. Other than the policeman and the few specks of dust, however, nothing seemed even slightly out of the ordinary.

'Cindy? Miss Carter?' a male voice said, right at her elbow, and for the moment Cindy forgot altogether the woman on the floor. She turned instead to find a handsome, if slightly overweight man in a dark business suit standing at her side.

'I'm Mike Dillon, from the Athens office,' he said, extending one hand toward her. 'We met once before, some years back, in New York. I don't know if you will remember me.'

'Oh, hello, Mike Dillon. And yes, of course I remember you, it's good to see you again,' she said, smiling.

'They sent me to fetch you,' he said, pleased to think she had remembered meeting him. 'I'm sorry I'm a bit late. Greek traffic, you know.'

'I do remember the Greek traffic. And it's very kind of you to take the trouble to pick me up, but, really, it was not at all necessary. I can manage a taxi on my own.'

Mike Dillon took her arm in a proprietary manner. 'Now, now, we can't have our visiting reporter, our ace reporter, finding her own way about the city of Athens. Not on her first day in town, surely?'

'I assure you I am entirely used to finding my own way around in strange cities. And I am a writer. A features writer, for the supplements,' she corrected him. 'Which hardly qualifies me as an ace reporter. An ace anything, for that matter.'

'You're doing that interview with Professor Landos while you're here, aren't you?' he said. 'The one Mister Baker set up. So, it was important enough to send you all the way from the New York office to do that rather than letting someone here handle it. I would say that makes you a reporter. An ace reporter, presumably.'

The pique in his voice made altogether clear who he thought should have been assigned the interview in her stead. 'Can I get your bags?' he asked on almost the same breath, giving her no opportunity to respond to his remarks.

'Oh, my bags. There they are, right there, on the porter's trolley,' she said, pointing. 'The two brown leather ones on the top and the off-white overnighter.'

He tipped the porter, apparently rather less than what the porter had expected, or so his disappointed glance at the coins and his frustrated huff said. Dillon got the bags she had indicated, holding a suitcase in each hand and tucking the overnight bag under an arm.

'Come this way,' He told Cindy. 'I left my car at the curb just outside, if the airport security people haven't hauled it away already. They sometimes get over zealous.'

'Oh, that woman, I think she may have . . . ' Cindy started to say, remembering Miss Perfection, but when she glanced back, attendants in nursing uniforms were already lifting Miss Perfection onto a stretcher and the policeman and a couple of passersby were dutifully collecting the things that had spilled from her purse (how could that tiny purse have held so much, Cindy could not help wondering?) And that man, a few feet away, was he staring at her? But when she looked again, he had averted his eyes. Just another would-be masher, she thought, dismissing him as quickly as she had noticed him.

Dillon had paused in mid step when she had started to speak. 'Yes?' he asked, looking back at her and seeming impatient with any delays. 'You were saying?'

'Oh, never mind,' she said, 'it looks like everything is under control.'

Cindy dismissed the incident from her mind and followed him toward the exit. She tried to deny to herself that there was some satisfaction in seeing Miss Perfection lose both her balance and her dignity, but the satisfaction would not be denied.

So much for those elegant travelers.

* * *

They had made it all the way to Omonoia Square, the very heart of downtown Athens, before a heretofore quiet Mike Dillon said, out of the blue, 'If I ask you a blunt question, will you give me an honest answer?'

She blinked. Athens was its usual kaleidoscope of color and confusion. It was not so much the number of cars that made it so breathtaking to the casual observer, but rather the way Greek men drove, as if their lives depending upon getting there ahead of everyone else, no matter where 'there' might be or who else.

She had rather been enjoying the circus that was Athens traffic, and was surprised out of her enjoyment of the passing scene by the brutal question. 'Why of course I will, why shouldn't I?' she said.

They were stopped at a light just then. He turned to give her a long cold look before he asked, 'Are you here to replace me?'

'I . . . Me?' she fairly sputtered 'No, absolutely not, why should I be intending to replace you? I told you, I'm here for two weeks on an assignment, that's all.'

'To write a series of articles on Athens, for the tourists?' He looked skeptical.

'Yes, exactly,' she said, wondering what had made him so prickly.

He sighed and said, 'It's been done, you know, a thousand times or more.'

'Yes, you're right, of course, I do know that,' she agreed. 'I can only suppose they wanted a fresh point of view.'

She managed to meet his gaze evenly, without blinking, but inside, she was thinking, *he's right, it has been done, if not a thousand times, certainly plenty and then some.* And if it was a new slant they wanted, would it not have made more sense to use someone local, who lived here, who knew the city's underbelly, so to speak? Someone like Mike Dillon.

But if that is so, then why exactly am I here, she wondered? Only to do what had sounded like no more than a throw away interview with an old college professor of Mr. Baker's? Why send her all the way here from New York City, just for that? But if was not for the interview, and not for the travel pieces, then why on earth had she just traveled halfway around the globe?

The light had changed. Horns sounded behind them. Mike drove obediently forward, no longer looking at her, seemingly not interested in her answer, though she could see that he looked more than a little petulant as he negotiated his way through the traffic.

'I can't actually answer for the boss,' she said over the noise of the other cars, answering her own questions as well as his. 'This is what he told me to do, and I am here to do it.'

'Ours not to question why,' he said,

without looking at her.

'Exactly,' she said. 'However silly it sounds, and you are right, it does sound silly, doesn't it? But mine is really not to question why, as you say it. I'm just a lowly worker bee.'

'No, of course you can't question the boss when you're told to do something. We're just little cogs in the wheel, both of us.' He seemed more resigned than satisfied with her answer. 'Well, whatever, they have certainly done you up royally,' he said, driving around the corner and pulling up in front of the hotel.

The Grande Bretagne was the acknowledged dowager queen of all the hotels in Athens, and called by many 'a crossroads of the world.' If there was anyone in town of any significance, sooner or later you were sure to run into him here, at the hotel bar. Everyone went there. Everyone, at least, who was anybody.

'Mr. Baker's secretary made the reservations,' she said, somewhat lamely, even a bit embarrassed. She was thinking, but did not say, that the secretary must surely have known how much she was supposed to spend, and no more. A week at The Grande Bretagne almost certainly cost more than the fee she was getting to write those pieces. Probably more than her monthly paycheck came to, for that matter. Which certainly struck her as odd. It seemed to give her visit an importance that until now she had not attached to it.

'However it happened, someone did indeed do right by you,' he said, more cheerful now. 'Very much right, I should say. About as grand as Athens gets.'

She gave the front of the hotel a dubious glance. 'It does look a bit much,' she said.

'Oh, I'm just being a spoilsport,' he said. 'Look, I'll tell you what, it's Friday, and it's after noon already, and to be honest, I have plans for a long weekend. I was supposed to go sailing around some of the Greek isles, starting today. I would have been on the Aegean right now, frankly, if I hadn't been asked by New York to pick you up, and I'm planning on rectifying that situation as soon as I can.'

'I can't say I blame you. I think I would rather be sailing myself.'

'Right. What I was going to say is, why don't you treat yourself to a couple of day's relaxation and call me at the office when I'm back, on Tuesday, okay? I promise, I will have a car and driver set up for you, everything you need, in fact, and you can exercise that fresh point of view all you want, and with my blessing.'

He sounded still a little annoyed, but his smile was genuine enough, and he was quick to hand her luggage out of the trunk to the uniformed doorman who appeared at the curb as if by magic.

'Thanks,' she said, smiling her best to enter into the friendlier spirit of things. 'Where are you off to, if I may ask? If anywhere in particular?'

'Mykonos,' he said, and made a moué. 'Or maybe not. I've got a friend with a yacht, so I'm told that's where we're headed, but with no assurances that it is where we will actually end up. You know how the Greeks are about specifics.'

'Umm, I don't, but I get your point. And I will call you on Tuesday, first thing, I promise. Have a great weekend.' She was tempted to ask if she couldn't come along. Mykonos, or wherever the yacht happened to go, certainly sounded more appealing than a couple of days in a downtown Athens hotel, knowing no one, and with nothing to do. But, of course, there had been no invitation to join him. Not yet, at least. And she certainly could not invite herself.

If he had meant to extend an invitation, however, it got lost in the shuffle of bags. 'Thanks,' was all he said. 'You too.'

And with that he was gone, his little blue car quickly vanishing into the inevitable horde of cars circling about the square. The door man had vanished too, with her bags. Cindy shrugged, checked to make sure she had her shoulder bag, and made her way into the lobby, to the registration desk, where a young man in a hotel uniform waited to greet her with, 'Welcome to The Grande Bretagne.'

While she filled out the necessary paperwork for him, her thoughts were in a muddle. It had not occurred to her that her arrival here was going to arouse any hard feelings with co-workers. Hopefully, by Tuesday, Mike Dillon would be over whatever had caused his unhappiness. It was not how one wanted to start out on an assignment.

But surely, Mykonos, or just a sail about the blue Aegean on a private yacht, was the sovereign cure for the blues, wasn't it? So, by the time she saw him again on Tuesday, he ought to be in fine spirits. Oughtn't he?

★   ★   ★

As it turned out, she had been given not just a single room at the hotel, but a small suite, a bedroom and a sitting room with a lot of over-gilded furniture, and brocade draped windows, one to each room, that looked out onto a quiet and well shaded back street.

She was grateful at least for that back street. Athens could get very warm, and without sunlight spilling into the room, it would stay cooler. And at least she would not have the incessant rumble of Omonoia Square to keep her awake half the night. Greeks were a late night people, as she recalled.

By the time she herself got to that suite, her bags were already there and had even been unpacked. Her clothes were hanging neatly in the bedroom closet. The little overnight bag, tactfully still closed on the assumption that it would contain her more private possessions, rested on a bench, upholstered in a ghastly maroon satin and sitting at the foot of the bed. The porter, who had presumably brought the bags up, and the maid in a black dress who must have unpacked the suitcases, stood at attention by the door.

She tipped them both, remembering just enough Greek to thank them, hoping that their delighted smiles did not mean that she was over-tipping. She set her purse upon a convenient chair and took a closer look at the sitting room in which she was standing.

Pride of place clearly went to a desk by the window, a precious quasi-French piece that one supposed was meant to serve as a writing post (the secretary must have mentioned that when the reservation was made) and which she doubted would serve at all for that purpose, and certainly not with the dinky lamp that sat atop it and radiated barely enough light to illuminate the desk's surface. She would have to talk to the manager about at the least switching that lamp for something more utilitarian. Or, there was a floor lamp over by the sofa, maybe she could move that over, and not have to deal with the manager?

She glanced at her watch. It was 2 o'clock in the afternoon. If she remembered correctly from that earlier, long ago visit to Greece, there would be no chance of having dinner before nine or even ten in the evening, and it had already been hours since the coffee and soggy croissant that had passed for breakfast on her flight. Lunch, which was also served late in Athens, suddenly sounded very inviting, and then just maybe she would take a nap before she thought about where to have dinner, and did something about that desk lamp.

She had worn a simple cotton shift for the flight (she found herself remembering, with renewed resentment, Miss Perfection's lovely Chanel suit) and it would surely serve for lunch in the lobby, but she was not much inclined to go anywhere without some repairs to her makeup.

When she checked, she found she had nothing but a tube of lipstick in her shoulder bag; she remembered then: the rest of her makeup was in the overnighter. She found her keys in her purse and went to the overnight case at the foot of the bed, trying to ignore that ghastly maroon satin. She discovered the moment she tried the key in the lock that the case was not hers.

'Bother,' she said aloud. She stared down at the case for a moment, thinking back. Yes, of course, it must have somehow gotten switched in that confusion in the airport. The bags had already been on the trolley when Mike Dillon had arrived. And before she had fainted, Miss Perfection had carried an overnight bag as well. Cindy had even noticed at the time that their two cases were very similar.

This must be Miss Perfection's then and the cases had simply gotten swapped around in the confusion of the moment, when she had fainted.

A simple enough mistake and one which could be easily enough corrected. She had only to find out Miss Perfection's real name and the bags could be switched back, and no harm done.

Except, when she searched for one, there was no identifying tag on the over-nighter. Not on the handle, the customary place, nor could she find one attached anywhere to the case's surface.

Even that was not particularly alarm-ing. Some travelers did not like to put their identification on the outside of their bags, just in case. So, surely there would be something inside to tell her who it belonged to. A name, an address, even a telephone number. She could not very well go about asking for Miss Perfection.

Only, if the identification tags were inside how was she to find them, without getting the bag open? She rattled the keys in her hand. She had learned before, from unfortunate experience, that these things did not always have the sturdiest of locks. It took nothing more than a little prying to spring the lock.

But prying with what? She rummaged through her purse and found nothing there that looked suited to the task. She went back into the sitting room, and at the bar there she found a long handled cocktail stirrer.

Which, when she tried it, did the trick. One end under the rim of the overnighter's lid, a little push, and it popped open as easily as you please. She lifted the lid, and gasped, taking a step back in astonishment.

The case was filled with neat little packets of money, rows of them, side by side. She picked up one of the packets and riffled through it. It was made up of one hundred dollar bills. Ten of them. A thousand dollars, then, in that single packet. She looked again at the contents of the overnighter, at the rows and rows of packets, nesting on top of one another, and did a quick calculation.

Good Heavens, even at a conservative estimate, there must be a hundred thousand dollars here. In cash, plain and simple.

Or, maybe not so simple. She put the

packet of bills back on its stack and left the lid up. She did not really know the applicable laws, but she was almost certain that there were laws against carrying this kind of cash from one country to another. If American laws did not prohibit the money from going out, surely Greek laws covered its coming in.

Which meant, someone, Miss Perfection, it would seem, was breaking the laws, and big time too. Which meant, well, what exactly? Smuggling of some sort, certainly. Maybe drugs. Whatever it was, it suggested nothing that could be regarded as legitimate. It was hard to think of a legitimate reason to carry a bag full of cash. Not this much cash, at any rate.

But what was she to do with all that money? She thought of calling the local police, but she was a stranger here. A stranger with a suitcase full of surely illegal money. Who was to say the local police would not start by arresting her, and sorting everything else out from that point?

Well, stranger she might be, but she was not without local resources. She got her address book out of her purse and looked up the number for the local office of Columbine.

She had actually given the telephone operator downstairs the number, and heard the phone answered on the other end, 'Columbine Magazine, Athens branch' before she remembered that Mike Dillon had said he was going away for the weekend. Had he said whether he was going back to the office before he left for his sailing trip, or not?

Damn! How was she supposed to find him on an unnamed yacht somewhere on the Aegean?

3

'And Alexei is not aboard?' Mike Dillon was asking at about that same moment.

'I am afraid not, sir,' the captain replied, giving a slight bow. 'But I was instructed to do everything I could to see that you are comfortable. Would you like a drink to start?'

'I . . . ' Mike hesitated, glancing at his watch. It was only a bit after two. *Oh, what the hell,* he thought, *I've got the weekend off. And surely the regular rules do not apply on a yacht anyway.* 'Sure, a gin and tonic would be nice. If that's doable.'

'Very good, sir.' The captain snapped his fingers and a steward appeared at his side as if my magic. 'A gin and tonic for Mr. Dillon. And use the private stock.'

I could get used to this, Mike thought. 'Oh, by the way,' he said aloud, 'Where are we going, anyway?'

'You did not know?' the captain seemed

surprised. 'We are headed for Mykonos, sir, unless you have somewhere else in mind?'

'No, no, Mykonos will be lovely. Or anywhere, really,' Mike said, dropping into one of the deck chairs, savoring the warm Greek sun on his face. The steward was there in what seemed no more than a moment or two later, bearing a tall, frosted glass on a tray, which he extended in offer. Mike took the ice cold glass and, nodding his thanks to the steward, who glided noiselessly away, sipped from it happily.

Yes, he thought again, *it would be very easy to get used to this.* He must remember to thank his host accordingly, when he got back to Athens.

But, why isn't he here, he wondered? It was so unlike Alexei not to be on hand.

★   ★   ★

Apparently Mike Dillon had not intended to go back to his office before leaving for the weekend.

'Sorry,' the voice on the other end of

the phone said, 'Mr. Dillon is gone for the weekend. I'm Robert, his assistant. Perhaps I can help you?'

'I . . . ' She hesitated. 'I don't know. It's Cindy Carter, Cynthia Carter, from the New York office.'

'Yes, Miss Carter, welcome to Athens,' Robert said. 'I had the impression Mike was going to see you settled into your hotel before he took off. Did he not show up?'

'Yes, he did, thank you, but . . . well, you see, I've got a problem and I'm not sure just how to deal with it.'

At the other end, Robert waited patiently for her explanation, saying nothing. 'It seems there was some confusion at the airport.' She said, rushing ahead. 'And I have got someone else's bag.' She hesitated and added, 'Well, an overnight case, actually. And, presumably they have mine.'

'No problem. Why don't you just bring the case here, and I'll deal with it. I'll call Lost and Found at the airport and explain things to them.'

'I . . . I don't think I can do that,' she said, cutting him off. She'd had a sudden and unnerving image of herself, carrying a hundred thousand dollars around in an overnight case, in modern day Athens, even for long enough to get in and out of a taxi. She felt sure she lacked the courage to do that.

'I see,' Robert said, in a voice that made it plain he did not see. That was followed by a thoughtful silence. 'Would it perhaps be better if I came there and got it?' he asked.

'Yes, but . . . ' She wasn't even sure if she should mention the real problem on the telephone. What if he called the police and she ended up being arrested all the same? Then she had a brain storm. 'Look, does the magazine have any connections with the embassy?' she asked.

'The embassy?' She could hear the surprise in his voice. 'The American embassy?'

It had suddenly occurred to her that this was who should be handling this business. Surely this came under the heading of diplomatic problems? 'Yes, of course, the American embassy. Someone in the diplomatic corps, I think is what I need?'

'I see,' he said again, in the same voice

as before. Another silence ensued. 'Am I to understand there is something problematic about the bag you've got?'

'Yes, there is, but . . . well, it's not something I want to discuss on the telephone.'

'I see,' he said for a third time, but this time a bit more optimistically. 'Look, I'll tell you what, just by coincidence there is someone here who might be able to help, or at least to give you some advice. She's an old friend of mine. Her name is Emily. Emily Gardner. Maybe she's the one you need.'

'Yes, if I could just speak to her, please.'

'Actually, she was just leaving,' Robert said. 'Why don't I ask her to pop over to your hotel? It's hardly out of her way at all and I'm sure she won't mind in the least. What room are you in, by the way?'

'Six oh three. Do you think perhaps . . . ?'

There was a muffled conversation at his end, apparently with his hand over the mouthpiece. He came back in a minute. 'Six oh three, right?'

'Yes, that's it.'

'Miss Gardner says she's on her way, she says she should be there within twenty minutes, half an hour at the most. Will that be all right?'

'Yes, thank you. I . . . '

But the line went dead before she could say anything more. It seemed he thought the subject was settled.

Which, she supposed, it was. Or, and this was the more likely explanation, he was busy, and she was an unexpected complication to his day.

In any event, she thought, replacing the receiver on its cradle, whoever this woman was, this Emily Gardner, she must be a person of some importance. Which meant she was surely someone who could take responsibility for an errant suitcase full of cash, without getting arrested by the local police.

Unfortunately, it also meant that, at least for the present, her plans for lunch were out the window. She was committed now to staying in her room, at least until Miss Gardner showed up. She looked around in the hotel suite and found a box of welcoming chocolates, and ate three of them while she waited, carefully wiping her fingers on a tissue she found in the bathroom. She had no more than discarded that in the bathroom's wastebasket when someone knocked at the suite's door.

She was surprised, not only by how quickly the knock had come, but she would have supposed a visitor would check in at the desk downstairs and they in turn would call to tell her she had company.

Of course, she had given Robert her room number, and coming directly to her room was certainly more discreet than announcing herself at the desk downstairs. Without really knowing, she rather imagined discretion was a good thing to exercise in a situation like this. But how would her visitor have known that? Unless, of course, she regularly exercised discretion. Some people did. People in government positions usually did, surely.

The woman at the door was small and rather a nondescript sort, neither young nor old, dressed in a conservative gray suit that almost matched her hair and her eyes. The sort of person you could meet one moment and not remember well enough to describe the next. Only her eyes hinted at the keen intelligence behind them: hard and bright, they regarded Cindy now like the eyes of an inquisitive sparrow.

She had a billfold in her hand when Cindy opened the door and before either of them spoke, she held it up so Cindy could clearly see an ID card: some sort of government identification with her picture on it, but it was gone before Cindy had time to register exactly what else it said. In any case, it looked official. And she had seen enough to know that the information on the card was mostly in Greek.

'Emily Gardner,' the woman at the door said, dropping the billfold with the ID in it back into her purse and stepping inside. She was careful, however, to close the door behind herself. 'And you must be Cynthia Carter?'

'Yes, but you can call me Cindy. Everyone does.'

'I understand there is some problem involving a mix-up with your bags. Something you did not want to discuss on the telephone?' Miss Gardner said.

Cindy led her visitor into the bedroom. The overnight bag was still sitting where she had left it, on the maroon satin bench, lid up, its contents plain to see.

'Would you want to talk about that on the telephone?' Cindy asked. 'To a stranger?'

4

Emily Gardner stared long and hard at the money. 'No, I suppose you are right. And you came by this, how?' she asked finally, turning to give Cindy a questioning look.

Cindy described for her the scene at the airport: Miss Perfection, her faint, and Mike Dillon's arrival. 'I think it might have been seeing the policeman come into the terminal that caused her to faint,' Cindy said. She had come up with this explanation while she was waiting for her visitor to arrive. 'She seemed like she was in perfect control up to that point, but looking back, I think it was a very fragile control. She must have been frightened. And when she saw him . . . ' She let her voice trail off.

'When she saw the policeman, you mean?' Emily suggested. 'Yes, perhaps she thought he was there for her.'

'Exactly. That money tells me she must

have been up to something, something nerve-wracking, I should think. But he wasn't? The policeman, I mean. He wasn't there for her?'

'I will check, but I rather doubt it. If the police had been aware of anything amiss, we . . . others, certainly . . . would have heard of it. But, yes, you would have to be nervous, would you not, carrying money like this around. I know I would be.'

'I think anyone would be,' Cindy said. 'Anyway, that happened at just the very same time when Mike showed up, and he got my bags off the porter's trolley, only he must have taken her overnighter instead of mine. They did look much alike, and I'm afraid I was not paying very close attention at the time, so I simply did not discover the switch until I got back here. When I tried to unlock the case, in fact, and my key didn't fit. That's when I first realized it was not mine.'

'I do not suppose there is any kind of identification with the case?' Miss Gardner asked.

'Not that I've seen. None on the

outside, at least. To be honest, I didn't really look for anything inside, not after I saw all that money.'

'Let us do that now, why do we not? It might solve the entire problem,' Emily suggested. She hitched up her skirt and, kneeling by the bench, began to lift the packets of money out onto the bed, counting them as she went.

'I get one hundred thousand dollars,' she said when the case was empty. 'And nothing else to be seen. No identification, I mean. Which makes sense, I suppose. If you were smuggling in this kind of money, you would hardly want to advertise your real name, would you?'

'Then it is smuggling, you think?'

The pause before answering was so brief as to hardly register at all. 'I should say so,' Miss Gardner said. 'Smuggling of some sort, at least.' She put the money back into the case, looked at the lid, and looked hard at the catch Cindy had pried open.

'I forced the lock,' Cindy said in an apologetic voice. 'I had no key, you see, and I didn't know the money was in there. Not until I had it open.'

'No problem. These locks are pretty cheap. In any event, I happen to know someone who can fix it so that it looks as good as new. They will never know you even saw inside.'

'Then you do know how to get it back to its rightful owner?' Cindy ventured. 'If rightful is even the correct word.'

Emily, still kneeling by the bed, grinned up at her. 'That is a nice play on words. Yes. I think we will do just what Robert said originally, contact Lost and Found at the airport. Oh, I will not exactly take the case there. After all, we would not want some clerk to catch sight of what is inside it. In which case, human nature being what it is, the money is likely to disappear into thin air, do you not agree? No, I will just leave a message there that it has been found, and let someone come to me for it.'

'Come to you where?'

Emily gave her a slanted look. 'There is a small NATO office locally. Not far from here, as a matter of fact. But you are to forget you even heard that mentioned. In fact,' she stood up, dusting off her skirt unnecessarily, 'I think the best thing for you would be to forget this incident altogether. I expect we will find that your case has already been returned to Lost and Found. If it has, I will have someone drop it off right away. And if it has not been found . . . well, I do not know exactly what you were carrying in yours.'

'Nothing like that, I assure you.' Cindy indicated the money. 'Just some makeup, a nightgown. Overnight sort of things. Well, that's why it's called an overnighter, isn't it?' She gave a nervous laugh. 'Nothing I can't replace readily at any department store, is what I mean to say. Don't worry about that. I'm just glad to have this,' she gestured at the open case on the little maroon bench, and the piles of money, 'off my hands.'

Emily leaned down and closed the lid, managing to get the damaged lock to hold, if none too securely. 'Are you going to want some sort of receipt?

'I don't think I need one. Do I?'

'Yes, I think it is best if you have it,' Emily said. 'We will keep everything above board, to be safe.'

She went back into the sitting room, carrying the case with her. Crossing to the hideous French desk, she found a piece of paper in one of the drawers and scrawled some words on it. 'I have made the receipt just for the case,' she said. 'Which I have stated is unopened. That way, if there is any trouble down the road we have covered our tracks.'

Cindy blinked, startled. 'Trouble? But why should there be any trouble? The money's all there, and if we're going to let them think I didn't see inside, I don't see what there is to worry about.'

Emily turned away from the desk. 'Miss Carter, it is hard to think of any innocent reason why anyone should be carrying this much cash around with them, would you not say?'

'Yes, I suppose you're right. It must be part of something illegal. But if you're asking them to claim it from you, then surely I am free and clear?'

'Exactly. It removes you from the equation. For the most part, in any event. But if there was anyone else at the airport at the same time, and surely someone was supposed to receive this case, then they might very well have meant to do so there. They must have seen this woman faint. They must have seen you, and the porter, and Mike Dillon coming to meet you, carrying your bags out to his car. I shouldn't think they will have too difficult a job figuring out who got it by accident, will they?'

In her mind's eye, Cindy saw again that stranger at the airport, and the impression she'd had that he was looking at her. But the odd thing was, she had paid him so little attention that she could not if her life depended upon it have described him.

'No, I should not think they would.' Cindy thought for a moment. 'I hadn't thought of that, someone seeing me there. Do you suppose I should change hotels?'

Her visitor thought briefly as well. 'No, we do not want to give the impression that you are worried about anything. Which you would not be, if you had not opened the case, right? No, just carry on as you normally would. That way you will be less likely to call attention to yourself.'

'Call attention to me? But, what are you saying? Do you think I am in any danger?'

'Hmm. I think not. Let us hope not, in any case. But when you are talking criminal activities, one cannot be entirely certain of anything. Where money is involved, this kind of money certainly, people are likely to do all kinds of outrageous things. I will tell you what, though, if it will set your mind at ease, I am going to have someone keep an eye on you, just until the cases are switched back.'

'A bodyguard? But surely that isn't necessary.'

'Do not worry, he will not be intrusive. You probably will not even see him yourself. It will simply be someone who can handle any problems if any should happen to come up.'

'Thank you. Miss Gardner . . . '

'Emily.'

'What do you think this was all about, anyway?'

Emily gave her a grin and made her way back to the door, carrying the overnight bag and leaving the receipt atop the desk. 'I would say with any luck, you and I will never know. A little unsatisfying, I suppose, but safer that way.'

She gave Cindy a mock salute and was gone, the door closing softly behind her. Cindy might almost have thought she had imagined the brief visit. Except that the case, with its worrisome contents, was gone.

The case. Thinking again of that, she crossed to the little French desk, checked the receipt that Emily had left there. Yes, it was for one overnight bag, unopened, and with a reasonable if terse description. And with the receipt was a card, like a business card but with no business establishment or address on it.

Nothing but a name, Emily Gardner, and a telephone number.

Cindy took the time to tuck the card carefully into her purse, glad to have it. Emily Gardner had inspired confidence in her brief visit. She had also made Cindy aware that however neatly she might dispose of the case and its contents, there was still an unbreakable connection between it and her.

And now, she thought, there was still time for a quick lunch, and if she ate dinner a bit later than she had intended, she could even have that nap beforehand.

First, however, she had some things to buy. There would surely be shops in the lobby, at least for the most essential things. The rest, she could get tomorrow.

★　★　★

Emily Gardner paused outside of the hotel room door, taking several deep breaths and giving herself time to steady her nerves. Her hands were actually shaking, although she had been able to disguise that fact while she was inside.

For all her nervous state, though, she had to laugh softly to herself. She had done it.

One hundred thousand dollars. And she had actually pulled it off. No one would have suspected a thing. Even better, she had knowledge beyond what many had. She knew who had mistakenly gotten the money. She knew who Cindy Carter was, and why she was here, in Athens, which had nothing to do with writing travel pieces.

Knowledge was power. Information was a commodity, to be bought and sold, traded or bargained for. Worth far more than the money in the case she held in her hands. Though certainly by the time she had managed things, assuming they went the way she intended, at least a portion of that money would be hers.

She laughed again, this time aloud, but not loudly, and hurried toward the elevator.

5

Cindy remembered The Grande Bretagne's bar from her previous visit. It looked entirely unchanged. She knew you could get lunch, or tea and scones, or coffee, or a drink, or, really, pretty much anything you wanted at any time of day or night. In addition to which, it was one of the rare bars in Europe that a single woman could walk into without feeling resented. Most European bars were intended for men, but not this one. Not, at any rate, exclusively, though at a glance she could see that the men in the room still outnumbered the women

Yes, there were the same clusters of men at the little tables, and one table made up of what she supposed were The Daughters of the Greek Revolution, hair stiff and waxy, eyes dark and frankly assessing her as she paused in the doorway. So at least the women were here, however much the men might resent it. And those Daughters did not look as if they would be easy to evict, from anywhere.

What was surprising was that for all of its eclectic nature, the room still managed to have the look of some Old Boy's club in London. And, of course, there were the men at the bar, she would have sworn the same men she had seen there before: journalists and diplomats and, for all she knew, a spy or two. Yes, almost certainly a spy or two if she knew The Grande Bretagne.

For a moment as she stood in the doorway she allowed herself to play a childhood game, trying to guess what each of the men at the bar were. But after a moment, she decided she was being silly. What did she care about spy business? It surely had nothing to do with her. She looked away from the bar, and around the room once more.

And, yes, there also, watching her step hesitantly into the room, was the same man whom she had seen a little while before in the lobby, when she had been purchasing some night cream from one of the lobby shops. His blazer was an odd olive green, which rather made him stand out amid the somber grays and blacks most of the Greek men in the room wore.

But after she had noticed him in the lobby, she would have sworn that he had left the hotel by the outside door, exiting onto the street.

Apparently he had not, though, because here he certainly was, his eyes hardly leaving her the whole time, even though he pretended to be reading a book that was propped on his table in front of him.

She found an unoccupied table not far from the bar and, when the waiter came, ordered a salad and a glass of wine.

'Retsina?' the waiter asked.

By which he meant the resinated wine of Greece. An acquired taste, she already knew, but one which she should probably acquire if she was to be here for a few days. It was hard to find French wines anywhere.

'Yes, of course,' she said, resigned to her resinated fate. She thought fleetingly of Paris, where even the vin de maison, the house wine which every restaurant and boite carried, would be refreshingly cool and easy on the palate.

Well, this was not Paris, and it was not likely to become Paris, however much she might wish for that.

The waiter had barely left when a man suddenly seated himself across the table from her. She had not even seen him approach. One minute, that chair was empty, and the next, a stranger was seated in it, leaning toward her across the surface of the table. A handsome man, she thought, in that Greek way, all beard and piercing eyes. A somewhat portly man, more muscle it seemed than fat, but tall and sturdily built. He almost did not look Greek in fact. Did she know him? She had a fleeting impression that she had seen him somewhere, recently. That idea teased her consciousness, but when she tried to focus more clearly on it, it had slipped away.

'You are Miss Carter, the American, are you not?' he said, and when she nodded, he said, 'I am Alexei Christophorus. I am a reporter.'

'And have you come to interview me?' She asked with a smile. She hardly thought she was important enough for that sort of attention.

That was apparently an opinion he shared. He laughed silently and open-mouthed at the suggestion, revealing gleaming white teeth; no, she thought again, he is not Greek. But what then?

'No,' he said, 'No interview. I just wanted to get acquainted. In case. Well, anyone new in Athens is of interest, do you not see? Especially a beautiful young woman.'

'You're very kind,' she said, blushing.

'Not at all. In any event, I should say, there might be occasion for an interview down the road. One never knows. In the meantime, I simply wanted to introduce myself. Here in Greece, no one stays a stranger for long.'

She understood then. He was the 'someone' Miss Gardner had mentioned, who would be keeping an eye on her. 'Well, you're more than welcome to join me for lunch, if you would like, but I'm afraid you will find me very disappointing material.'

'I doubt that,' he said, and his eyes

made a serious compliment of it, in that way that Greek men had; so maybe after all she had been mistaken.

'And thank you for the invitation,' he quickly added, 'But I have already had luncheon. I was on my way to the bar, where I will go now. I just wanted to take the opportunity to make your acquaintance.'

'I'm glad you did,' she said, and meant it.

And with that he was gone, although she watched him go and he did only go as far as the bar. He glanced back once, and she dropped her eyes, but she was grateful to know he was there. Only, he had said he was a reporter, but a reporter for whom? Had he mentioned a newspaper? She thought not. Didn't reporters always like to boast of their newspapers?

Still, she was glad to have him close at hand. Especially since, as she looked around the room, she saw the little man with the olive green jacket once again staring in her direction. He saw her glance at him, and went back to pretending to read his book.

She thought, when she left the bar not quite an hour later, having finished lunch, that she had left the little green man behind at a table not far from the one where she had sat. Only, no such luck, there he was again in the lobby, this time flipping his way through a magazine off the news rack and most demonstrably not paying her any mind.

She would hardly have been surprised to finding him waiting on her floor when she stepped off the elevator there, but he was not. She hesitated briefly outside her room. If she waited for the next elevator, might he be on it?

She decided all of a sudden that she really did not want to know the answer to that question, and let herself quickly into her room, but she double-locked the door behind her and, on a whim, took Miss Gardner's card from her purse and laid it on the desk top, by the phone.

She wondered briefly if she should mention the stranger to Mr. Alexei Christophorus and decided she did not want to return to the lobby just at the moment to see if he was still there.

Anyway, he almost certainly must have noticed the olive green jacket, as she herself had done. Alexei Christophorus did not strike her as the sort of man who missed much.

Instead, she slipped her dress off and, hanging it carefully in the closet, turned back the coverlet on the bed and slipped into it, planning on her nap.

Despite her fatigue, however, it was a long time before she fell asleep. She lay there listening to the sound of the elevators from the hallway, and every time she heard one stop at this floor, heard the doors woosh open, she strained her ears for the sound of footsteps approaching her door.

Even when she finally fell into a fitful sleep, she dreamed of a man in an olive green blazer.

6

Cindy's intention was to spend a lazy weekend lolling about the hotel, with perhaps an exploratory stroll outside to one of the many sidewalk cafes surrounding the square. In her memory, Athens cafes were always interesting, frequently entertaining places, even for a woman, though there was little doubt that women were . . . well, women were not quite second class citizens here, as they certainly were in some places, but at the same time, there was little question Greece was a man's world.

Reality, in the form of some cabin fever, caught up with her all too soon, however. By midmorning of the following day, she was already beginning to tire of her room, nice though it was, albeit in its own kitschy way.

The back street visible from her suite's windows was indeed a quiet one. Though she went to the window often, she never saw a single human, although a car did drive up and down it one time, presumably with a human at the wheel. In any case, whatever that driver was looking for, he or she apparently did not find it. The car went quickly back the way it had come and disappeared into the river of traffic at the far end of the street.

Had he been looking for a parking space, perhaps? The curbs were parked full, but no one that she saw came or went from any of the cars. Probably they belonged to the neighborhood residents and Saturday morning was a time for most Athenians to sleep in.

She went down to the bar, ostensibly for a late breakfast or early lunch, which she could just as well have ordered delivered to her room. Really, her intent was merely to get out of the room for a while.

She was relieved to see no one in an olive green blazer, neither in the lobby nor in the bar, though she did catch sight once of Alexei Christophorus at the bar, engaged in a spirited conversation with someone who looked very much like a reporter. More like a reporter, in fact, than Mr. Christophorus did, or so she thought. But, really, who was she to say what a reporter might or might not look like?

She sat at the same table she had occupied the day before (reserved, she wondered for single women?) and had a freshly baked croissant, some cheese and a small salad. Within an hour, she was back in her room, which by now had all the charm of a prison cell. She felt sure she could not endure it for two more days, until Tuesday.

And, really, why should she treat herself like a prisoner? The busses to Delphi, which left from the nearby square, made the trip down in a couple of hours, and returned the next day. Surely the concierge downstairs could arrange a car and driver for her (she had no desire to test herself with those Greek drivers) who could get her there in time for an afternoon of sightseeing, and bring her back the following day.

Nor had there been any specific time set for her meeting with Professor

Landos. Who was to say it could not as easily be done early on Monday? Then it would be out of the way, so to speak, and she would be free to concentrate on her other business, the travel pieces, when Mike Dillon was back in his office on Tuesday. Although admittedly his remarks had managed to dim her enthusiasm for that project, which had now begun to seem to her more like busy work than a real assignment.

Suiting action to thought, she rummaged through her shoulder purse and found the slip of paper with the Professor's address on it. There was a phone number written on the paper as well and she briefly considered whether she ought to telephone ahead of time to let him know she would be there on Monday.

She decided otherwise. For one thing, there was the language barrier. Mr. Baker had not said if the Professor spoke English, or if he did, how well. And telephone conversations could test a rudimentary knowledge of a foreign language, as was hers of Greek. It was easier when you were face to face with someone; facial expressions and hand gestures got one through a lot of tough spots, it seemed to her.

Moreover, in her experience, though it was admittedly limited when it came to doing interviews, surprise was sometimes a valuable asset. Anyway, until she was actually there, talking to the man, this plan of action was still all very tentative. She could easily enough change her mind at any time and simply go shopping on Monday instead.

But if she called him ahead to make an appointment, why then she was committed to that plan, wasn't she? No, she decided she would keep everything casual, spur of the moment, as it were, and see how things panned out. It gave her more flexibility.

7

So, by early afternoon, she was in Delphi, having been driven there by an affable young man whose English was flawless and whose knowledge of history was good enough that he was able to point out to her on the way there the very spot on the road where, it was said, Oedipus had that fateful meeting with his father. Of course, for all she could say, he was making that up. How would she know?

She had a late lunch at what was clearly a family operated taverna in Delphi, and then strolled down to the sacred groves. What was left of the Apollo's temple, where Greeks of old had consulted the Oracle, stood there. Not much was left of it now, only a few columns and a basin, but she almost thought she could hear those ghostly voices still.

From there, she climbed the trail that led up to the old theatre where the acoustics were allegedly so perfect that if an actor stood on the right spot on the stage, a whisper could be heard all the way to the rear of the auditorium. She stood in the back row, and wished she had someone with her to test the theory. Still, in her head she could hear those wonderful lines from Sophocles' Electra, as they might have been spoken from this very stage:

' . . . Dreaded Hades, sweet Perso-
phone
Faithful Hermes, servant of death,
And ye Eternal Furies, Children of Gods,
Those who see the murderers
The adulterers and the thieves, come
near, I urge you!
Avenge ye my father's death, and bring
my brother home.'

It was not yet evening when she came back into the town of Delphi. Still plenty of time to visit the museum there, to see once again one of her favorite pieces from antiquity: the wonderful bronze of The Charioteer. She stood and stared at it as she had done before, and it seemed to her once again that those glass eyes stared back at her. Who was he, this handsome young man driving the chariot, captured by the sculptor not while in the race, else his robe would have been billowing? Perhaps it was in the moment of victory celebration that the sculptor had portrayed him. Even the robe itself was a mystery. At that time most athletes would have competed and been portrayed in the nude, yet he was clothed as chastely as any virgin bride. Because, some said, he was a household slave, and so to show him unclothed would have been regarded as unseemly. Whatever the reason, she rather liked him this way. It seemed to make him in some way exceptional. As, of course, the statue itself was.

She had dinner at the same taverna where, this being her second visit and Greeks being the people they were, she was welcomed not as a tourist but as an old friend.

She rose before dawn the next day to make her way once again to the groves, this time to see the sun rise. The cliffs that rose above the grove, white and steep, were known to the ancients as The Shining Ones, and were said to be home to the gods. There was a moment, just at dawn, when the rising sun struck the cliffs and turned them, for a few minutes only, into enormous sheets of gold. Watching this spectacle, she little wondered that the ancient Greeks had thought this the home of the gods. Certainly there was no mystery as to why they had called the cliffs The Shining Ones.

After her dawn visit to The Shining Ones, she returned to her hotel for a hearty breakfast, and afterward met her driver once again, as scheduled, for the trip back to Athens. By Midday on Sunday, she was once again having lunch at the bar at the Grande Bretagne, and still wrapped in the dreamy splendor of Delphi.

Early Monday (early by Athenian standards, which meant late morning to anyone else) she set out to visit the Professor and do that interview. She started by consulting a map of Athens that she had found in the bookstore in the lobby.

The address Mr. Baker had given her for Professor Landos turned out to be one of those twisting narrow streets that ran out from the Plaka, the city's old neighborhood, in the shadow of the hill upon which stood the Acropolis. And, at least so she surmised, studying the map, it was not far at all from her hotel.

She started out on foot, but finding the address she had been given, however, had proven more of a challenge than she had anticipated. First off, there were the street signs: all of them, predictably enough, in Greek. But the address Mr. Baker had written down for her in New York City, had been in English. Independence Street, the note said. Number thirty two. The map she consulted had given the street's name in both Greek and English, but the signs she found in the Plaka did not. They were in Greek only.

She thought her limited Greek was at least up to that much, but such had not proven to be the case. She had quickly given up as a lost cause the idea of finding the address herself and on foot. The Plaka, as she perhaps should have remembered, was nothing more than a warren of streets and alleys going off of one another in an endless maze, a veritable mouse nest.

A friendly cab driver, however, and one, blessedly, whose English was impeccable (in her experience, this was more often true than not in Athens) had been more than happy to translate for her, and bring her virtually to the professor's door, if not quite all the way.

The alley that led up to his apartment building was too narrow for the large American car (a Plymouth, it said on the dashboard) he was driving to negotiate, and he'd had to leave her instead at the corner, with assurances that number thirty two was only a few feet up the dark, narrow passage to which he had pointed.

'Just there, Kyria, you cannot miss it,' he had assured her before driving off and leaving her to her own devices.

He had been right, however. She found the door easily enough, not more than twenty feet from where he had put her down at the entrance to the narrow alley. Though perhaps calling what she found 'the door' was over-gilding the lily a bit. It turned out to be nothing more in fact than a rough plank of wood in the stone wall, but it had the right numbers splashed somewhat sloppily on it in bright orange paint, something that might have been done by an enthusiastic but not very gifted child.

Standing outside that door, she could see that the gloom of the alley, a kind of perpetual twilight, surrendered to bright daylight only a short distance ahead of her, and out of curiosity as much as a desire to put off the moment of actually meeting the Professor, she walked those few feet further. At the alley's end, she stepped out into one of those little squares that were often hidden and could sometimes surprise the explorer in the city, offering a moment's respite where none would have been expected. So very Greek, she found herself thinking, stumbling upon this little island of sunlight after traversing the dimness.

To be honest, there was not much to her little square. Windows looked out and down from all four of its walls. No doubt the apartments represented by the rows of windows depended upon what was really nothing more than an over-sized light well for any hope of day light within. Directly across from the narrow alley by which she had entered the square, was what was presumably a bar or a coffee house. A single forlorn table and a pair of chairs stood on the rough cobblestones in front of this establishment.

One of the chairs was occupied just at the moment, and for a long moment she stood frozen, half in and half out of the shadows of the passageway. Surely she had seen that same man only yesterday, had she not, at her hotel? He had been wearing an olive green jacket at that time, and she was sure she had seen him both in the hotel's lobby and in the bar, pretending to read a book but in fact, she had been sure of it, watching her. Was he perhaps following her? But no, how could he be, since he was here when she arrived? It must be nothing more than coincidence, she told herself.

For that matter, could she really be certain that this was even the same man? At the moment he was turned sideways to her, reading a newspaper, and from this distance, she suddenly was not entirely sure. He looked like the same man, in a different jacket this time, a gray one. If she were to be honest, however, it was the jacket more than the man which she had noticed the day before. It had been so unlike the usual black or gray that Greek men generally wore.

In any case, regardless of what he was wearing, this man seemed to have no interest in her. He had apparently not even noticed her arrival on the scene. He did hold the paper aside once, briefly, but it was to glance up, not in her direction.

He seemed to be looking at one of the windows above. She followed his gaze, but it was impossible to say from where she stood which of those windows interested him. If indeed any one of them particularly did. For all she could really say, he might have been glancing up at the sky. She even looked up herself for a moment, automatically, though there was nothing there to be seen. Not a single cloud marked the bright blue expanse. Clouds were apparently not permitted in Greek skies, or only rarely so.

Before he could turn his head in her

direction and see her standing just within the square (and why should that matter anyway, she wondered, but she did not want to think about the answer to that question) she turned and made her way back through the gloom of the alley to the rough wood of the door with its orange point proclaiming it to be number thirty two, and knocked on it.

There was no immediate reply, and no sound from within, and she knocked a second time, louder, hard enough to hurt her knuckles on the unfinished wood. This time the door opened, but only the smallest crack. Wide, frightened looking eyes regarded her through the narrow opening.

'Yes?' a voice asked from within.

'I'm looking for Professor Landos,' Cindy said, glad to hear English spoken with no more than a trace of an accent.

'Is he expecting you?' From somewhere beyond the face at the door, came peals of childish laughter. From the sound of it, she guessed there were two of them, a boy and a girl.

'Yes, I,' she started to answer, and

corrected herself. 'Well, no, he was not exactly expecting me today, in fact. To be honest, we had not set up an exact time for meeting. I am Cindy Carter. I was to interview him. Mr. Baker, Mr. Theodore Baker of the magazine Columbine in New York City, sent me. The professor knows him. Or did know him, at any rate, in the past. I believe Mr. Baker was a student of the professor's, some years ago.'

The young woman at the door — Cindy had determined that much at least, that she was a woman and young — looked over her shoulder, as if she were seeking approval. Apparently she got it, from someone. A moment later she swung the door open. As she did so, Cindy was sure she heard another door being closed somewhere above.

'First floor, first door,' the young woman said, stepping aside. The concierge, Cindy thought. At least that is what she would be in France, though she did not actually know what they called them here in Athens. In fact, the young lady had looked not quite like anything so much as a sentry guarding a door.

Now that Cindy got a good look at her, she realized too that the girl was clearly nervous about something. And she was indeed young, not more than eighteen. Pretty, in that Greek way: oval faced, wide eyed, her dark hair pinned back severely.

Yes, she was decidedly nervous, Cindy thought, glancing at the trembling hands that still held tight to the edge of the door. Well, perhaps the Professor did not get many visitors. Mr. Baker had said he was somewhat eccentric. Maybe she was frightened of him.

From a few feet beyond the girl at the door, the children laughed again. Yes, as she had deduced, two children, a boy and a girl, Cindy saw, neither of them more than six or seven. They regarded her with unabashed curiosity. It seemed that visitors were a rarity here. Or perhaps the rarity was visitors who spoke English.

'Hello there,' Cindy said to the children, sending them both for some reason into renewed paroxysms of laughter. Behind her, the concierge closed the outside door firmly and pointed to a flight of rough-hewn steps circling up one wall.

'First floor, first door,' she said again.

Meaning, Cindy thought, for whatever reason, I am not supposed to linger down here. She gave the young woman a brief smile and a nod, and another to the children, and made her way up the stairs to what she would have called the second floor but which Europeans insisted upon calling the first. There, she knocked on the first door she came to. It opened at once, as if the person inside had been just waiting there for her to knock.

The man within stepped behind the door to let her come in. The apartment into which she entered was dark, gloomy really, even allowing for the gloom of the alley outside. The only light to be seen came from a window in the far wall. At a guess, she thought, a window that looked out onto the little courtyard she had seen moments before. Could this, she wondered, be the very window at which the seated man had stared so intently? But that of course was only fancy on her part. He might have been looking anywhere for all she could say.

The man inside the apartment now

stepped forward from behind the door, out of the shadows there and into the dim light. 'You are Miss Carter, yes?' he greeted her.

'I am,' she said, holding out her hand. 'And you must be Professor Landos.'

He ignored the offered hand and instead made a gallant little half bow from the waist. 'At your service, Kyria. Can I get you anything? Some tea, perhaps? Or would you prefer a glass of wine? Greek wine, I am afraid.'

'A cup of tea would be nice,' she said; she wasn't quite ready for another glass of resinated wine. 'If it is not too much trouble.'

'It will be no trouble at all. I have had the kettle on as it happens, thinking I might soon want a cup for myself,' he said. 'It will only take a minute or two to brew. Please, make yourself at home.' He indicated the apartment with a grandiose sweep of his hand.

The professor was a small man. For some reason, she had been expecting someone tall, but he could not have been more than five two or five three at the most, austere, in a suit perhaps a size too large for his thin frame.

'Thank you.' She started for the small sofa against one wall and instead, on a whim, went to the window and, pulling the curtains back, looked out.

Yes, she was right, it did look down upon the little courtyard, and there below her was the same man, sitting at his table and still reading the newspaper. As if he sensed her eyes upon him, he glanced briefly up at the window. She stepped back from it and realized as she did so that as dark as the apartment was, he could not possibly see into it. Was that why it was so dark, she wondered?

'Is he still there?' the professor asked from behind her.

Startled, she turned and found him standing only a few feet away, bearing a tray that held cups and saucers and a diminutive china teapot. He smiled, looking a trifle amused at her surprise.

'The man with the newspaper?' she asked. He nodded. 'Yes, he is. Do you know him?'

'I know who he is, though we have

never been formally introduced. Please, will you do the honors?' He set the tray and its contents atop a small table in front of the sofa. 'I am afraid there is no cream, but I have added sugar already. I hope you do not mind.'

'Not at all.'

She took one more glance out the window and saw that the watching stranger was on his feet, talking to someone. As she looked down on them, the second man walked away, and within a few paces was out of her range of vision.

For a moment, she had the eerie impression that the second man was Alexei Christophorus.

8

But, no, she quickly thought, surely she was mistaken in that. Why would Alexei Christophorus be here, at the same time as she was visiting the professor, and talking to the man who had yesterday been wearing a green coat? If this even was the man who had worn the green coat. Surely Alexei Christophorus's job had been to guard her, not to collaborate with those who were watching her. If, that is, anyone was. Of which she was not altogether certain.

And, really, if she were to be honest with herself, at this angle it was hard to be sure of either man. As for the second one, the newcomer, she had seen little more than the top of his head, thick with wiry mostly gray hair. Her impression that it was Mr. Chistophorus had come as much as anything from the way he had walked, a very stately sort of procession, as if he were in a parade.

Now that she thought of it, though, and if she were to be honest with herself, she had seen that same prideful step in many of the men here in Athens. No doubt it was a Greek thing. As for the other man, the one who had been seated in the square when she arrived, she was sure now she must have been mistaken about him. It made no sense to suppose he was the same man who had been watching her so intently the day before. And, as she had already concluded, he could hardly have followed her here, since he had been sitting in the table in that little square when she arrived. It seemed she was just being foolish. That business with the overnight case and the stash of money had spooked her more than she had realized.

She made the effort to dismiss both men from her mind, and brought her attention instead back to the tea tray and her host, who was obviously waiting for her to 'do the honors,' as he had so quaintly put it.

She sat at the brocaded sofa behind the table and taking up the china pot, poured out two cups and handed one to him. He had taken a seat directly across from her. He took the cup from her with an unsmiling nod of thanks, his keen bright eyes watching her steadily and a bit unnervingly.

She took a sip from her own cup and quickly discovered that the tea was sweet indeed, overpoweringly so. As, really, she ought to have suspected, she scolded herself. That too was a Greek thing. Tea and coffee were always served almost unbearably sweet. She sat the cup carefully back on its saucer.

'Now then,' she said, leaning forward slightly, 'I am supposed to be interviewing you, although I must confess, I don't really know in connection with what. Mr. Baker said you had some news you wanted to share. Why don't we start with that? What was it you wanted to share with him?'

'How is Teddy, by the way?' the professor asked instead, leaning forward as well.

She had to think for a moment. She had never heard her boss addressed as

'Teddy,' but his name was Theodore, so it made sense at least. She made a mental note to try the Teddy label on him when she got back, just to see his reaction. With luck he might not fling her out a twenty-second floor window.

'He's fine,' she said, and raised an eyebrow slightly to indicate that she was still waiting for an answer to her previous question.

Now that she was here with him, however, the professor seemed reluctant to broach whatever the subject was that had brought her. The silence grew a bit lengthy, and awkward. She had determined she would wait until he was ready to open up to her before she said anything further. Maybe after all this visit would prove to be nothing more than a waste of time. She rather suspected that would be the case, but she had promised Mr. Baker, and she meant to stick it out.

The professor cleared his throat. 'Perhaps I should begin by asking you a question. Do you consider yourself patriotic, Miss Carter?'

The question was certainly one that

surprised her. 'I suppose I do, yes,' she said. 'To be honest, I had never really thought much about it.'

'I suppose none of us really do think about that, as a general rule,' he said. 'It is rather one of those things we tend to take for granted, is it not? And yet, let us say your country was threatened, what would you do?'

'Threatened? By war, you mean, or . . . ?' She left that question hanging.

'But of course,' he said, and now he seemed to be thinking aloud, or talking to himself rather than to her. 'Teddy would not have sent you, if he thought you were a fool or . . . ' His voice trailed off.

'Professor Landos,' she said, 'I might as well be frank with you, I don't quite know myself why Mr. Baker, Teddy, as you call him, sent me here. To see you, I mean. He is not a man, I shouldn't think, to do things for no reason, but nothing he said suggested the reason for this visit. Not that I could see.'

He stood up, so suddenly that he bumped the little tea table and made the china on it rattle. A bit of tea sloshed from her cup onto its saucer.

'Miss Carter,' he said, 'you asked me before if I knew the man outside, watching this place. Yes, you need not look so surprised, he is indeed watching my apartment, if you had not already guessed that. No doubt he made note of your arrival, as he will note your departure when you go. But in order to answer your question, I must first tell you a story. Do you mind?'

'Please, I would be delighted,' she said, and added, 'Do I need to take notes?'

'No, the notes have already been taken,' he said. He went to the desk in one corner and, opening a drawer, took a large manila envelope out of it. He regarded it briefly and glanced at her. 'The notes are in here. When you leave, I hope you will take them with you. Back to New York, to Teddy. He will know what to do with them. If indeed there is anything that can be done.'

'I'll do as you ask, of course,' she assured him.

'But first . . . ' He hesitated. He walked to the window and looked out, and shook his head. Finally, he turned his back on the window, facing her once again. 'He is gone,' he said, and added, 'for the moment. He will be back, though.'

'Will he? Can you be sure of that?'

'I would bet money on it. He has been here for most of the day. Most of the week, in fact. Only yesterday was he not out there, watching. I can but assume he must have had some other assignment yesterday.' He paused, and cleared his throat.

Cindy was thinking, I may know what yesterday's 'assignment' was. And realized, as she thought it, that she was taking things altogether too seriously. It would not do to get caught up in the professor's paranoia. There was almost certainly a logical explanation for everything, that did not involve people watching apartments for some nefarious, if unspecified, reason.

'After the war,' he said, seeming to have lost interest in the other subject, 'that would be the Second World War, I mean. After that conflagration, Athens was a shambles. Much of Europe was, of course, but I do not refer to damaged buildings only. We had those too, but what in some ways was even worse, here we had what some have described as a power vacuum. No one really knew who was in charge. The Nazis had been defeated and driven out, but the Communists had been very quick to try to take their place. And then, of course, there were the Greek patriots, who wanted no outside power ruling us, who wanted an independent and free Greece governed by Greeks. Do you know any of this history?'

'Very little, I'm ashamed to say,' she admitted.

He gave her a wan smile. 'Few do know it, outside of Greece. It does not matter, really. I am only trying to fill in some background for you.' He paused again, and seemed to be marshalling his thoughts, choosing his words. 'I was a member of the Greek resistance. I was only a boy at the time, mind you. Many of us were. Many of the grown men had been killed in the war, or taken away by the retreating Nazis. Still, young as we were, we thought we were fighting for the good of our country. We also believed we shared a common dream of the future for Greece. What we did not realize at first was that the resistance had been well infiltrated by the Communists, and much of what we did was counter-productive in terms of the Greece we dreamed of for that future.' He paused again and looked down at her scarcely touched cup. 'Is the tea not to your liking?'

She had quite forgotten the tea. 'Oh, no it's fine, really,' she said, lifting the cup to take another sip and determinedly resisting the urge to make a face at its overpowering sweetness.

As if reading her thoughts, he said, 'For many, our tea is too sweet. It is the way we Greeks like it. Perhaps because there has not been a great deal of sweetness in our lives over the last few years.'

'No, no, really, it is not too sweet at all.' She forced herself to take another sip.

He was apparently satisfied with that. 'There was one man,' he said, returning to his narrative, 'we knew him by his code name, Ares, and we thought he was Greek, but it turned out he was not. He was a Russian, a dedicated communist, and his real name was Kouzinov. He had infiltrated our little resistance group, and over time, he brought about the deaths of many of the true patriots. Apparently he had a death list. Later, I learned that my name was on that list.

'In time, however, and as you can see before he got around to my name and had me murdered as so many others had been murdered before me, his true identity was discovered. Then, before justice could be done, Ares, or Kouzinov, if you will, disappeared, utterly. No one knew where or how. He was just here one day, and the next, he was simply missing. He had vanished.

'Some believed that justice had been done after all. The story went round that his treachery had become known, and he had himself been murdered by some members of the resistance. Do you think it cold of me to speak of murdering a man so off handedly?'

'I quite understand,' she said.

'Do you? I wonder?' He paused for another long moment before continuing.

'In any event, no one mourned him, I can assure you of that cold fact. Anyway, rightly or wrongly, for years, that was the story we all believed, that he was dead. We thought it was over, you see, not just the war, but the struggle for the soul of our country. We had our Greece, after all, the Greece we had all dreamed of, one governed by Greeks, by patriots.'

He had been pacing the floor as he talked. Now he came back to where Cindy sat, picked up his cup and drained it of tea.

'I believed it, too,' he said. 'Perhaps because I wanted to believe it, but believe it I did. Until a year ago.' He paused again.

'What happened a year ago?'

'I saw him, with my own eyes.'

'So the stories were untrue? He was not dead, then?'

'Kouzinov? No, I saw him, I tell you, right here in Athens, walking right through Omonoia Square, as big as life. Oh, he had taken pains to change his appearance. He had a beard now, and he had put on some considerable amount of weight. He had been thin during the war and after. But then all of us were. You understand?' Cindy nodded. 'But no matter what he did to change his appearance, he could never have fooled me. I recognized him the instant I saw him.'

He sat his empty teacup down with such force she half expected the china to shatter. 'I recognized, and followed him,' he said, speaking now in a ferocious whisper, 'followed him to a house not far from here, in the Plaka. A house where he seemed to be altogether at home. He had keys for the front door, I saw him let himself in. There were others inside as well. I heard their voices, men who greeted him in a familiar way. What I am trying to say is, it was clear he was not just passing by. He belonged there, in some sense or another. He was entirely at home there.

'But why, I wondered? What did it all mean? Why had he suddenly come back from the grave, to Athens, of all places? The one place where surely he was most likely to be recognized?'

'But perhaps the one place he knew the

best,' she said. He nodded his approval.

'Yes, yes, you are right, the one place he knew intimately, where he could do the most mischief. And it was clear to me that he was indeed up to some kind of mischief. But what mischief, that was the question? So I began to watch, not him especially, but that house, because it was clear to me that something was afoot there. I went to observe the house at all hours of the day and night.' He paused and glanced in the direction of the window, but he did not go to it as he had before.

'And?' she prompted him. 'What did you learn from your observations?'

'For one thing, the house was a veritable beehive of activity. There were people coming and going all the time, at all hours. He, the house, was visited, and often, by men that I knew to be Communists, many of them the same men who had in the past plotted the overthrow of the freely elected government here. And not just here, either. By this time, Greece had a friend. A friend known to much of the free world. Your country, Miss Carter. The United States.'

'Professor,' she started to say, but he seemed not even to hear her, so engrossed was he now in his story.

'You must understand, I was not without resources that I could call upon. I still had many friends from the old days, from the resistance. Some of them by this time were in positions of some importance. I called them together, we met here, in this very apartment, and they were as alarmed as I had been. So we set out to see for ourselves what these people were plotting. Because it was obvious to all of us that they were plotting something.

'But, it was not this time the overthrow of our government that they intended, not in the near future, anyway, though that remained as always their final goal. No, this time they were after a much bigger target. The United States.'

She stood up then, brushing off her skirt, thinking by this time she had surely heard enough. 'Professor, many people over the years have made a target of the United States, but my country is still standing.'

'You think I am just an old fool.' He smiled mirthlessly. 'I tell you, there is a plot afoot, and a fiendishly clever one. You see, I employed the same stratagem they liked to use, I planted a mole. In time, I got very nearly the entire story.'

Almost despite herself, she was still curious to hear where all this was heading. 'Which is?'

'In a nutshell: their plan is to murder an important political figure here in Greece. But the assassin will be made known almost at once, captured, betrayed by the very people he thought were his friends, his comrades in arms.'

'But, if he is to be captured at once, what then would be the point?'

'The point is, when he is found, he will have a large sum of money on him. American money, in cash.'

She tried to keep her face blank, but she could not help thinking of the suitcase full of cash she had mistakenly intercepted the day before. But surely that was nothing more than coincidence. It could have nothing to do with his incredible tale.

'The implication will be obvious,' he went on.

'Will it?' she asked, so lost in her own thoughts that she did not immediately grasp the meaning of his remark.

'Yes, of course,' he said. 'It will look to the world, to the Greeks, at least, as if the Americans hired him to commit the murder.'

She gasped aloud. 'But why should we want to do that?'

He laughed drily. 'For no reason whatsoever, obviously. But reason rarely applies in cases like these. If you know them at all, you know that the Greeks are a passionate people. We are quick to love and to hate. To laugh, and to anger. Perhaps too quick. The Greek press will be full of the story for weeks, the news broadcasts, everything. The Greek government will sever ties with the Americans, they will have no choice but to do so, to break off diplomatic relations. Which means, we will once again have a political vacuum in this part of the world, and the Communists will be quick to rush in to fill that vacuum. Within a year, Greece will have become a Russian satellite. Ares, Kouzinov will have won.'

'And Kouzinov is . . . ?'

'The missing man,' he said with a sigh. 'Oh, that is just what I call him to myself. I know he is here. I know this is his doing. His fingerprints are all over it. But just who he is now, or where, that I cannot say. He has once again vanished, seemingly into thin air.'

'But the house, the one you were watching, isn't that still there?'

'That house is empty now. He has gone. They have all gone. Like puffs of smoke in the wind.'

'Maybe they have given up as well whatever they had planned,' she suggested, but that sounded lame even to her own ears.

'Or maybe the trap is ready to spring. If the plans have all been made, then there is no longer a need to make plans, do you not see?' He picked up the envelope he had left atop his desk. 'But with or without the plotters, the rest of it, the details, the names, the dates, all of it, everything I have learned, is in this folder. Here, take it with you,' he said, thrusting it at her. 'Take it to Teddy. Everything is there, all of the facts, their entire plot. What is more, I do know that it has already been put into play. This is why I told Teddy it was urgent. He has friends in Washington, in high places. He, or his friends, certainly, will know what to do with this information.'

She wondered how much of what he was telling her was true, and how much might be nothing more than mere paranoia. But her boss had asked her to come see him, and she was obligated to do nothing more than carry an envelope back to him to peruse. He, or his friends in Washington. And she knew her boss well enough to know at least that part of it was true. Theodore Baker did indeed have friends in Washington, people high up in the government. They could decide for themselves about its contents.

'Of course I'll do as you wish,' she said. 'But you promised to tell me about the man outside.'

'Oh, yes.' This time he did go to the window and looked out. 'He is not back yet. Perhaps he is gone for the day?'

Which meant, she supposed, that he had not really been watching this building, this apartment, at all, or he would hardly have left his post so early in the day. Paranoia. Yes, it could make one see all sorts of bogey men lurking about. 'You said you knew him,' she prompted the professor.

'I said I knew who he was,' he corrected her. 'In the old days, we thought he was just a close friend of Ares. But when we discovered that Ares was really Kouzinov, the truth became apparent. This man's name, the only one we knew him by, was Janus. The name, if you will recall, of the Roman's two-faced god. Janus was Kouzinov's bodyguard and right hand man. He still is, from everything I have observed. And the fact that he has been watching this building for some days means that not only did I recognize Kouzinov when I saw him that day in the square, but he must have seen and recognized me as well, though he showed no sign of it at the time.'

He turned abruptly from the window. 'And which means as well that you must exercise every caution, Miss Carter. They may have seen that you came to visit me today. They almost certainly would have seen you, and they will wonder why you came here, what I might have told you.'

She glanced down involuntarily at the manila envelope in her hands.

His eyes followed hers. 'I suggest that you leave that envelope in some safe place where they cannot get to it. Do not leave it lying about in your hotel room on the sixth floor of the Grande Bretagne.'

He smiled at her surprise. 'Oh, yes. I told you, I am not without resources. I needed to know a little something about who Teddy was sending to see me.'

'You might just have asked,' she said, a bit annoyed to think that people had been spying on her.

He ignored that. 'You must go,' he said. 'At once. Now, while Janus has left his post. With luck, he will not see you go. It is even possible he might not have seen you arrive, though I think that unlikely. Still, we must hope that is so. Trust me, it will be better all around, for all of us, if he did not.'

As he spoke, he was shooing her toward the door. 'Thank you for your time, Miss Carter,' he said, opening it for her.

'One question,' she paused to ask. 'This man, this Kousinov, does he have a first name?'

'Alexei,' he said. 'At least, that was the name he used in the long ago past.'

She frowned. Alexei Kousinov, Alexei Christophorus. Another coincidence? Of course, Alexei was not an uncommon name here. It sometimes seemed as if half the men of Greece were named Alexei. For all she knew, that was true of Russians as well.

'Go,' was the last thing he had to say to her, in a hoarse whisper. 'Go quickly.'

She had no sooner stepped through the open doorway than he had closed the door behind her, quietly but firmly.

When she had gone, the professor stood for a long moment staring at the door he had closed. Had he made a mistake, entrusting the papers to her? She was only a girl, so vulnerable looking, and so innocent of the world's evils.

And yet, Teddy would hardly a have sent a fool on this errand. He must have trusted her to deal with the responsibility, with the danger.

If, that is, Teddy took any of it seriously. The girl had not seemed to. Which made her even more vulnerable to people like Kousinov. Probably, she had never before dealt with people of his ilk. He wished to Heaven he himself never had. Once you have made the acquaintance of evil, however, you could never again un-know it.

He sighed and turned from the door. He had done all he could do. The rest of it was with the gods.

★　★　★

Definitely a crackpot, Cindy was thinking as she made her way back down the stairs. The two children were still playing in the courtyard below. They called noisy goodbyes to her as she went through. The same young woman saw her to the door and let her out. The alley outside was empty, no watchers lurking about. Surely the professor had only been imaging things.

Of course, it was too much to suppose that a taxi would be waiting when she emerged from that alley. She set out walking, hoping she could find her way back through the twisting maze of streets that made up the Plaka and all too aware that she could walk for hours before she found her way back to familiar territory.

Well, she reminded herself, if there was one thing the Plaka did not lack, it was tavernas. If worse came to worst, there was always a glass of retsina to be had. Even more than their super sweet tea and coffee, the Greeks loved their wine

She had walked no more than a half dozen blocks, however, before a green car, a little Italian Fiat, pulled up at the curb beside her and a window was rolled down in the rear.

'Miss Carter?' The woman inside called her name and learned toward the open window. 'Cindy?' Cindy recognized Emily Gardner at once.

'Miss Gardner, Emily,' she said, astonished. 'How did you find me, here?'

Miss Gardner sat back, as if afraid of being seen. 'Get in the car, quickly, before anyone sees you.' The rear door swung open.

Cindy climbed obediently in next to

Miss Gardner in the car's back seat and before the door had even fully closed, the car was already moving, like an impatient dog on a leash.

They had gone no more than a few feet, however, before there was a sudden, violent explosion that sent the little sedan rocking.

9

'What on earth was that?' Cindy exclaimed, but Miss Gardner paid her no mind. Instead, she leaned forward and said something to the driver in Greek, way too fast for Cindy to understand, though she thought she heard the Professor's name in the middle of it. The car shot forward with a grinding of gears, rounded a corner, then another, and Cindy realized they were going back the way she had just come.

Yes, there was the entry to the alleyway down which Professor Landos lived, where the taxi had dropped her — was it really no more than an hour or so earlier? A large cloud of gray and black smoke was billowing out of the alley. Cindy jumped out of the car behind Emily Gardner.

'No, don't,' Emily said, grabbing Cindy's arm when she would have braved the smoke and dashed into the alley. 'Let him.'

The car's driver, a tall, slim man,

clapped a handkerchief over his mouth and disappeared into the clouds of smoke. He was back in a moment, coughing and gasping for air as he stumbled toward them.

'Is it . . . ?' Emily asked him.

He shook his head, his face carefully expressionless. 'It's gone,' he said, coughing. 'The whole building is gone. Everything. Everyone.'

'But . . . there were two little children there,' Cindy cried, unable to believe that those lives were so suddenly gone. 'What happened?'

'A bomb,' he said. 'It looks like someone planted a bomb. Probably on a timer.'

But I was just there, Cindy thought. *Another moment or two and I might have gone as well.*

She suddenly saw the man who had been sitting in the square outside, and the other, whom she had only glimpsed from above. The one who had come later. She saw them walking away. Not together, but both had gone within a matter of minutes of one another.

Had they known? Was that what the

newcomer had come to tell the other one? What had Landos called the watching man? Janus? The two faced one. The earth suddenly seemed to tilt.

'Do not faint,' Emily Gardner said sharply, and Cindy suddenly realized she had been very close to doing just that. 'Get back inside the car, quickly,' Emily said, steering her toward it. 'Before anyone sees you. Especially not now. Especially not here'

The three of them clambered hurriedly back into the little sedan, and in a few seconds it was once again speeding away.

'But shouldn't we . . . we should call someone,' Cindy said. 'The police, or, or someone.'

'They are on their way,' Emily said, and indeed, Cindy could hear the blare of emergency sirens approaching. The driver took a corner on two wheels, then another. He seemed to be doing nothing so much as trying to get them lost.

Or get someone lost, Cindy thought. 'My hotel,' she said aloud. 'I must . . . '

'I do not think you can go back. Not there, I should say,' Emily said. 'The hotel might not be safe for you, just at the moment.' She leaned forward again to talk to the driver in that same rapid Greek. After a brief exchange, they seemed to have agreed to something, and Emily sat back again. She took the manila envelope that Cindy was still holding. In all the excitement, Cindy had forgotten entirely that she even had it.

'Did he give you this? The professor,' Emily asked, tapping the envelope with one finger

'Oh, yes.' Cindy stared at the envelope as if she had never seen it before. 'I was instructed to take it back to New York, to my boss.'

'You are not safe with this in your possession. More to the point, it is not safe. I will take care of it.' Emily Gardner's tone was flat, decisive. She put the envelope on her own lap, her hands possessively on top of it.

Emily knew, or at least had a pretty good idea, what was in the envelope. As a one-time member of the resistance, she had attended that meeting in Professor Landos's apartment, when he talked about seeing Kousinov. A meeting of which she had informed the Russian, and for which information he had paid her well. She had long ago traded her loyalty, had sold it, in fact.

Had she gotten Landos killed? Quite possibly. Kousinov had wanted to prevent the Professor from sharing with others what he knew. But Kousinov had been too late with his bomb. That information, too, she would sell.

In the resistance she had been known as The Manipulator, because that was what she did. To her way of thinking, anything you could influence was to be manipulated. So, not only had she known the names of her fellow members of the resistance, she had known their families as well, and where they lived. A man might disappear. The hills of Greece were dotted with caves where a man could hide for years if he chose, and those seeking him might never find him. But a man had needs that could not be supplied in a cave, not without outside help. And Greeks being Greeks, that help was almost certain to come from family.

A fool could search the hills and caves forever, but a much surer way of finding a man who had gone into hiding was to watch his family. Sooner or later, and most likely sooner, someone, probably a small child, because often this job was assigned to them, would steal out of the family home late at night, or very early in the morning, carrying a bag of food; cheeses, bread, perhaps figs, and a goatskin of wine or even of water. If you followed him or her, you would soon find your missing man.

Information was a commodity. She had sold it often to the highest bidder. Knowledge was power. The only power a woman like her could wield in a man's world. But it was a considerable power, because she had considerable knowledge. Now, for instance, she not only had the Professor's notes, but she knew who he had spoken to about his fears. She not only knew the American woman's name, but where she would be hiding, thinking she was safe. But, however it had come about, Cindy Carter was a threat to certain people. People who would pay any price asked to learn where she was.

Where Kousinov or his agents could find her, if they wanted to silence her. And they surely would want to do so.

10

Cindy wanted to argue with Emily over the envelope, but another part of her was glad to be done with the responsibility for whatever was in it. She had thought of the professor as a crackpot, hopelessly paranoid. Now he was dead, his building and everyone in it destroyed by a bomb. And if Emily was to be believed, she herself was in no little danger as well.

She thought again of the two small children playing in the courtyard. What kind of monster killed innocent children as if their lives simply did not matter? She choked back a sob and looked out the window to distract herself. They had left the rambling streets of the old town behind and were climbing a hilly street into a visibly better neighborhood.

'Where are we going?' she asked. Not, obviously, back to the Grande Bretagne hotel, that much she knew already.

'We are here,' Emily said. They turned

into a courtyard, its gates standing open, and came to a stop in front of a small apartment building.

'Where is here?' Cindy asked.

'It is a friend's apartment, which we are borrowing briefly. You will be quite safe. No one will find you here.'

'But, my things,' Cindy said. 'My clothes, my notebooks, everything. It's all still back at the hotel. I can't just leave them there.'

'We will get them, all of it.' Emily Gardner gave her hand a comforting pat. 'Do not worry, everything is going to be all right. Go with Richard. He will see that you are safe.'

Richard was, apparently, the driver. He had gotten out from behind the wheel and opened her door. Now he took her arm to help her out of the car. To her surprise she found that her legs were wobbly and kept threatening to give out on her, but Richard kept a firm grip on her arm. Steering her expertly, she thought a trifle hysterically, just like he had steered the car.

He escorted her up the steps to the

front door and fitted a key into the lock. Looking back, Cindy saw that Emily had already disappeared. On foot, apparently, because the little Fiat was still there, but its rear door stood open and the car was clearly empty.

Emily Gardner was already three blocks away, and running. Kousinov had to learn where the girl was, and quickly.

★　★　★

Inside, Richard led her up another flight of stairs, where a second key opened the door to what proved to be a large and well furnished apartment, one that only missed being luxurious. A man's apartment, she thought fleetingly: worn leather furnishings, books piled everywhere. It had a homey kind of disorder, the kind of disorder, she thought, that suited a man, a bachelor.

'You'll be safe here,' Richard said, echoing Emily's remark. 'There's a bar just over there, if you need a drink and I think you might, and the bath's just beyond that door, the kitchen is that way.'

He pointed the way to both. 'There's a balcony off this room, behind the curtains just there, but I would not stand out on it if I were you. To be frank, it is best if you are not seen period. In case anyone is looking for you. And I think if they are not already, they soon will be. But they have no reason to look here, unless someone just happened to see you. It's best not to take that risk.' He made as if to go.

'But I don't have a key,' she said. 'How will I get back in if I go out?'

'You won't need one,' he said flatly. 'Stay here. Do not go anywhere. Do not go outside especially.'

'But, where am I? Whose apartment is this?' she asked.

'It's mine. But for the present, at least, think of it as yours. I'll find elsewhere to stay, so you need not worry about that. You will be quite all right here. And safe. No one will find you here. As long as you stay inside.'

There was a writing desk near the window, with a phone atop it. The phone rang. After a brief hesitation he crossed the room and went to answer it. He listened for a moment in silence, and then said, 'Fine. I'll be there. In twenty minutes. Yes, I understand.'

When he had hung up the phone, he came back to where she was standing. 'When we picked you up on the street a little while ago, you were carrying a manila envelope. What happened to that?' he asked.

'Emily, Miss Gardner has it,' she said. 'She took it from me on the way here.'

He frowned. 'This envelope, it was something entrusted to you by Professor Landos, I assume?'

'It was, yes,' she said, a bit defensively because he almost sounded as if he were accusing her of something. 'But I thought surely it would be safe to let NATO have it.'

Steel gray eyes blinked. 'You thought Miss Gardner was with NATO?' he asked, surprised.

'Why, yes, I did.'

'Did she tell you that she was?'

'Yes, she told me . . . ' She hesitated, thinking back. No, Miss Gardner had not actually said she was with NATO, she had only mentioned a NATO office nearby. 'Are you saying, she is not? Not with NATO, I mean?'

'She is not. I am, but Miss Gardner is a minor functionary in the local government. At one time she was a minor functionary in the Greek resistance, which is how she knew Professor Landos. But truth to tell, Emily Gardner's chief interest is Emily Gardner, and especially her well-being.'

'But, if you know what she is like, why do you hang around with her?' Cindy asked. 'You were with her earlier, when you found me.'

'We hang around with her, as you put it, because we use her for various services, mostly for information, and no doubt vice-versa. Greek politics can be very complicated. We went by your hotel today and when we didn't find you there, she made a guess that you might have gone to see the professor. That's how we happened to be in the neighborhood when . . . well, when we found you.'

Cindy clapped her hands to her face.

'Oh, I've been such a fool.'

'No, you were tricked, by someone very skilled at it. Believe me, you are not the first person she has duped.' He thought for a moment and taking her arm, led her to a settee by the window. 'Sit, please.'

She did as he bade. He sat beside her, but carefully not too close. 'Perhaps you should tell me about your conversation with the Professor,' he said. 'Did he give you any clue as to what was in the envelope he gave you?'

'He didn't tell me names or dates, but he did explain the rest of it. And the money part I already knew of. Oh, Miss Gardner has that too. The money.'

'Money?' He repeated. Clearly she had surprised him again.

'I think I had better start at the beginning.'

'Yes, I think you should,' he said. 'And tell me everything.'

So she did. She told him everything she could remember, starting with her arrival at the airport (was that only three days before? It seemed like an eternity) and concluding with her visit to the professor and its aftermath. When she had finished, she said, 'And then you brought me here. What are we going to do now?'

'You are going to stay here, inside, as I have already instructed you. And, I? Just now,' he said, 'I have an appointment to meet with Miss Gardner, in one of the cafes on Omonoia Square. That was her on the telephone a few minutes ago. And since she called to make these arrangements, I'm guessing she wants to bargain over something. With luck, I may be able to get your envelope back. Though not the money, I should not think. And, no, don't feel bad about that, it's only money.'

'Only money?' she said, surprised. 'But there was a great deal of it. A hundred thousand dollars. I believe. That's not what I would describe as only money'.'

'Of course, you're right and I do apologize. I did not mean to sound dismissive. What I meant is that there are things at stake here far more critical than a bag full of money.' He got to his feet and started again toward the door.

'But what should I do?' She asked his retreating back.

'I hope you are going to do exactly what I told you to do. Stay here, and out of sight. Please.'

He paused again, half in and half out of the door. 'And don't answer the telephone,' he said.

With that he was gone.

11

Richard had no difficulty finding Emily Gardner when he arrived at Omonoia Square. She was at the nearest table when he drove up and left his car by the curb. She smiled at him as he crossed the sidewalk to join her, noting as he did so that she did not have the professor's envelope with her.

He dropped into the chair opposite her. A slim-waisted waiter approached, and veered away when Richard shook his head.

'I thought we were making a swap,' Richard said. 'The envelope for some information.'

'I got the information I needed from the envelope,' she said. 'In any case, Kousinov wanted to hold on to that for the time being.'

'So you're working for Kousinov now, are you?' he asked.

'I am working for myself, frankly. As I always have been. But that does not mean I cannot cooperate sometimes with the

Russians. I go where the air is freshest.'

'And where the pay is the best,' he said drily. 'Let us not pretend, Emily. So why are we here, then if not for the envelope?'

'Because I have something even better to offer you.' She leaned back in the wire chair and smiled across the little table at him. 'I think so, anyway, and I am pretty knowledgeable about international matters, I think you would have to agree.'

'You're clever, certainly, I'll grant you that much,' he said. 'So what is it that you think is so much better for me?'

'Kousinov,' she said simply.

That startled him out of his relaxed air. 'Kousinov? What do you mean?'

'I thought that would interest you,' she said with a knowing smile. 'Frankly he says he wants to defect.'

'Why would he?'

She shrugged. 'Who knows? You know how secretive they are about everything, the Russians. Maybe he has gotten wind of a demotion in store for him back in Moscow. His last two projects did not go so well. The money he was supposed to receive was lost and he failed to stop the

Professor from warning the allies. In the old Russia, that alone would have been worth a trip to a gulag, even for an agent as highly placed as Kousinov.'

Richard Cranston looked somewhat pointedly about the square. 'So, where is he then?' he asked. 'Kousinov? If he wants to defect, he has only to come right up to me.'

She took a long moment to answer. 'As I understand it,' she said, studying her fingernails, 'he is just about now boarding a train for Paris. Not, of course, under the name Kousinov.'

'Paris?' Richard said, startled. 'Why should he go to Paris?

'There has been a change in plans. Everyone's plans, as it happens. He will meet you there. This,' she pushed a small slip of paper across the table at him, 'is where he will meet you. It is the address of a café, near the opera. And, as I have been informed, he will defect there. Give himself up to you. On the day after tomorrow. Oh, and he will give you that envelope back at the same time. If you still want it.'

'Then I had better get moving,' Richard said, starting to stand. 'I'll need to be in Paris myself. Which means travel arrangements.'

'I am afraid there is one other detail he insisted upon,' she said quickly, before he could leave.

He paused, half in half out of his chair. 'And that is?' he asked, suspicious.

'Miss Carter,' Emily said. 'She must be with you.'

'Cindy Carter?' Richard frowned. 'But why on earth should she be with me?'

She shrugged. 'He says she can identify him. They have met, it seems. And I am sorry to say, Miss Carter was not included as a request, but rather as a condition of the meeting.'

'That will be up to Miss Carter, won't it? I can't very well force her to go to Paris with me.'

'Then you will have to persuade her, I am afraid. But I know you can be very persuasive when you put your mind to it.' She smiled up at him, a cat like smile. 'That is, if you want Kousinov.'

'Bitch.' He spat it out without thinking.

'Yes, I am,' she agreed, still smiling. 'A woman has to be, if she means to get ahead in a man's world.'

'And the money?'

'I have that.' She smiled again. 'Do not worry, it is safe. That too will be returned. So long as everything goes according to his instructions.'

He shoved his chair back so violently that it toppled over and fell to the sidewalk. He left it there and strode briskly back to his car.

She watched his retreating back, scarcely noticing the waiter who ran over to right the fallen chair.

How interesting, she thought. Richard has already developed some sort of attachment to Cindy Carter. Now how, she wondered, can I make use of that knowledge? Because she had learned long ago, everything she knew could be used in some way or other. It was simply a matter of finding out how to manipulate what she knew. She would find a way to use this knowledge, too, when the appropriate time came.

* * *

By Tuesday morning, notwithstanding the comfort of her temporary quarters, Cindy was once again suffering cabin fever.

Since Richard had dropped her off on Monday, she had seen no one, talked to no one. The phone had rung on three different occasions, but she had followed his instructions not to answer it. She had not stepped outside, not even to stand on the little balcony, though she had several times parted the curtains to peek out, wishing she could just go for a long walk, visit a café, anything to relieve her restlessness.

Monday afternoon she had wakened from a long nap to find her bags in the front foyer. Presumably Richard had gotten them from the hotel and brought them here while she slept and had left again without waking her. And, everything was there, he had missed nothing.

That, however, was as close as she had gotten to any kind of human contact. She did have one small triumph, if it could be counted as such: at least now she knew

Richard's full name. Richard Cranston, assuming that the mail in the living room desk was his. But that little discovery, though it had been a happy one, had still left all those hours to drag tediously by.

So, by Tuesday morning, she was fairly climbing the walls. And she had a perfect excuse, too, as she saw it, for going out. Whatever she had inadvertently gotten mixed up in, she was still a working girl, working for Columbine magazine, and they were expecting her to show up at the local office on Tuesday to start an assignment.

She found an address book in a drawer of Richard's desk and in that the telephone number for a taxi company. She used the telephone to make a quick call to order a cab. By nine o'clock Tuesday morning she had left a note for Richard, explaining where she had gone, and she was waiting outside when the taxi pulled into the court-yard.

She got into the cab and gave the office's address, all the while half expecting an angry Richard to materialize out of nowhere and scold her for not obeying his orders, but her departure went off with only one small hitch. As the taxi drove out of the courtyard, another car approached. It stopped and waited for her cab to make an exit before it drove into the courtyard. But she could not see where it went after that.

She looked back once as they passed through the wrought iron gates, wondering if she was making a mistake by leaving. Whatever restlessness she had suffered since she had been brought here, she had felt altogether safe. By venturing out into the world at large, she might well be leaving her safety behind. That, at least, had been what both Emily Gardner and Richard Cranston had hinted at, and the explosion at the professor's apartment had certainly underscored their warnings.

The truth was, even apart from the question of her safety, she nonetheless approached Columbine's offices with no little trepidation. Her meeting with Mike Dillon Friday had not been altogether a happy one, and she had no idea what to expect of this one. His instructions had been to call him, and here she was showing up in person.

Moreover, if one wanted to be critical, one could say she had botched the interview with the Professor. She no longer had the envelope he had given her, certainly. That had not been with the things left for her in the foyer. But would anybody at Columbine even know that?

The Columbine offices were on the third floor (the second, if she went by Greek rules.) To her surprise, she had no sooner announced herself at the reception desk beyond the double glass doors than Mike himself came rushing out of one of the cubicles to greet her with a big grin and a bear hug, his earlier pique seemingly forgotten.

'I guess there's no question who has the pull here at this publication,' he said, beaming at her like a proud parent.

'Pull?' She stepped back and looked up at him in confusion. 'What pull? I don't know what you mean.'

He laughed loudly and gave her shoulder a gentle slap. 'She doesn't know what I mean,' he said to no one in particular, winking. 'I mentioned to you on Friday — and casually, if I may say so — that someone locally could as well have done the travel pieces you were sent here to do, and, voila. Today it's my baby.'

She blinked, giving herself a moment for this to register. 'Well, that's . . . that's wonderful. I'm so happy for you,' she said.

And she was, wasn't she? But that was why she had come all the way here from New York City, that and the interview with Professor Landos. Did this change in the assignment mean she was to be bundled upon the first plane back to Manhattan, her tail between her legs?

Which fears he dispelled with his next words. 'Well, it's not like you are going to suffer any, either' he said. 'I mean, come on, a trip to Paris? To tell you the God's truth, I'd just as soon you did the travel pieces and they sent me to Paris, but who am I to complain?'

This took a little longer for her to grasp. 'I'm going to Paris?' she said. When he looked puzzled at her, she said again, but this time emphatically, 'I'm going to Paris.'

'Indeed you are,' he said, beaming again. 'And first class, too. First class flight, staying at the George Cinq, which is certainly as first class as Paris hotels get. Now, where are those tickets? Amy, have you got Cindy's travel documents?'

As it turned out, Amy, the pretty girl behind the reception desk, did. She was there in a moment, with a large white envelope. Cindy emptied the contents into her hand.

Yes, there was a first class plane ticket, on Air France, and a voucher for two nights at the George Cinq (well, a visit to Paris, but necessarily a brief one). And enough money, in cash, to ensure that she would not have to stint on wine and baguettes while she was there. A girl could do a lot in two days, if she put her mind to it.

She looked the documents over carefully and slipped everything back into the large envelope, tucking that into her oversized shoulder bag. 'The flight is today?' she said.

'Yes, this afternoon,' Mike agreed. 'In about three hours, as a matter of fact. Do you want me to drive you to the airport?'

She almost agreed before she remembered that her things were still back at Richard's apartment. She had seen no need to bring them with her.

'No, thank you,' she answered. 'I'll have to pick up my bags on the way and . . . well, it'll be simpler, really, just to grab a cab.' Simpler, certainly, not to have to explain about that apartment, or why she was staying there instead of at her hotel, where Mike no doubt supposed she still was.

She said hasty goodbyes all around, thanking Amy and again congratulating Mike, and hurried from the office. She would have to move right along if she wanted to get to the airport in time for her flight.

She was eying the curb outside for a taxi when she stopped dead in her tracks. A taxi already waited at the curb, and there, grinning and holding the rear door open was someone she recognized at once.

'Richard,' she said, duly surprised, 'what on earth are you doing here?'

'Waiting for you,' he said. 'Get in. We've got a plane to catch.'

'We?' She slid into the back seat and moved over to make room for him. He got in too, slammed the door, and gave the driver directions in Greek. The taxi roared away from the curb and plunged into the sea of cars circling Omonoia Square.

'I'm going with you,' he said. 'Orders. From on high.'

'Surely not for my protection?'

'Let's just say my boss and yours are old friends.' He gave her a quick wink

She was silent for a moment after that. He had not denied that he was going along to see that she stayed safe. Which meant, did it not, that she was still in some danger? She had thought that part of things was behind her.

'What are you thinking?' he asked. 'You look awfully serious.'

'I'm thinking, there is far more to Mr. Baker than I ever imagined,' she said frankly.

'I expect that is true. And once this trip is over, I would suggest you forget all about that,' he said. 'Some things are better left unsaid. Maybe even better forgotten altogether. For your sake, and for his. If you catch my drift.'

'I do, and . . . Oh, my bags' she said, suddenly remembering. 'They are still at your apartment.'

'Actually, no they are not. They are in the taxi's trunk already,' he said.

'You're very efficient.' She gave him an appraising look. And very attractive, she was thinking, but did not say. If one must have a bodyguard, there was something to be said for having a handsome one.

'I just learned about our trip this morning myself, when I got to my office,' he explained. 'I came by the apartment to fetch you and when I found your note, it seemed wiser just to pick you up when you left your workplace, and to bring your bags along to save time.'

'There is one thing . . . ' She hesitated.

'Yes?' He looked genuinely puzzled.

'Why?'

'You mean, why Paris?' he said.

'Well, yes, that too,' she said. 'But most especially, I mean, why me? If Professor

Landos is to be believed, this is a matter of great political importance. I'm no diplomat, nor even a politician. I could see your going, I guess, although I don't really know what your job is. But how am I supposed to fit into the picture?'

'It's . . . it is a bit complicated,' he said.

She looked toward the front compartment. The driver was paying them no attention, focused instead on the busy traffic outside, an endless whirl of cars, all of them seemingly on a collision course with every other car. Horns honked ceaselessly, fists were shaken out windows. The usual Greek driving manners, she thought wryly. One reason she had not even thought of renting a car while she was here.

'I don't think he understands English very well,' Richard said, following her glance at the driver. 'I tried him out before you left the Columbine offices.'

'I see.' She rolled her window down to let the noise in and sat back in her seat, turning a bit so that she was facing him. 'In that case . . . let me think, it will take us about half an hour to get to the airport, as I recall,' she said, lowering her voice to be safe. Even if the driver did understand English, and tried to listen to their conversation, the traffic noise through the opened window would make it very difficult for him to follow what they were saying. 'Is that enough time to un-complicate it?'

He shook his head and smiled. 'You cut right to the heart of it, don't you?'

'I guess you could look at it that way. The way I see it, however, is that, through no fault of my own, I seem to have been swept up into some sort of dire international conspiracy. I might have died in an explosion at the professor's apartment. And for reasons that are not yet clear to me, I am being whisked away from one assignment and sent on another, the nature of which remains a mystery. I'm going to Paris — not that I mind that, of course — and I'm going first class, which means all of this is indeed important to someone. And you — and Miss Gardner, so far as that goes — have both given me reason to suspect that my life may be in danger.'

'As it may well be,' he said in a somber

voice. 'I would most certainly not want you taking any of this less than seriously.'

'That being the case, I think that gives me ample reason to ask, what in the name of Heaven is going on here?'

He thought for a moment. She looked at his face sideways and decided that he was not simply being obstinate with his silence. He had the look of a man sorting things out in his head, trying to think how best to explain them. She waited patiently for him to do so.

'If you talked to Professor Landos,' he said finally, speaking slowly and with his own voice lowered as well to not much more than a whisper, which meant she had to lean close to hear him (and caught, while she was at it, a scent of fresh after shave, something masculine and spicy) 'then you know that there is a plot afoot to assassinate an important political figure.'

'Yes, someone in the Greek government,' she said, nodding her head.

'Not the Greek government, though that was the original idea,' he said.

'But, who, then?

'The plan now, as I understand it, is to assassinate someone in the French government.'

Her eyes flew open wide. 'And that's why we're going to Paris?'

'Yes. And because that's where a man called Kousinov is, the man who presumably hatched this assassination plot.'

'Kousinov. The missing man,' she said.

Richard looked puzzled. 'That's what the professor called him,' she said in the way of explanation. 'He seems to have disappeared. Again, as I understand it.'

He thought about that for a moment. 'Yes, I can see why the professor would call him that. Kousinov has disappeared more than once. But just now he is not really missing, though we don't know at the moment exactly where he is, except that he is in Paris. At least he was supposedly on his way there two days ago, so by now I suspect he is there, somewhere in that vast city. We don't know exactly where, however.'

'But, you're right, Paris is a vast city. An enormous one. How are we to find him, then?'

'We don't. But we do know where he is going to be. He will be at a certain sidewalk café in Paris, tomorrow afternoon. Where he will find us.'

'And we know that because?'

'We know that because Mister Kousinov has informed us he wants to defect,' he said. 'News that has people in several governments turning cartwheels, frankly. Yours not the least of them. And probably your Mr. Baker too, but it's best you forget I told you that.'

She took a deep breath. That was important news, if she was to believe what Professor Landos had told her. She had not, not when she met him a few days ago, but since then, much had happened to convince her.

'And this café?' she said. 'We know where that is, I presume.'

'We do. That is where he wants to meet with our representative.'

'But, I still don't understand. What has all this to do with me?'

He gave her a blank look. 'Kousinov requested that you be there. You are to be our representative.'

'Me?' Her voice went up. She saw the driver glance at her in his mirror, and quickly lowered it again to its near whisper. 'But that's insane. It's preposterous.'

'Preposterous or not, that was his demand. And it was a demand, too, not simply a request.'

'But, me? Why would he have asked for me? Whatever on earth for?'

'For identification purposes, as I understand it. He says you know him and you will recognize him. Understand, we know the name, Kousinov, but we have no face to go with the name. But he knows you. And it seems you know him, too.'

'But I don't.'

'Maybe not by that name, but you must know him by sight, at least. At some point in time you have met him. He says you will know him when you see him.'

'But, if he is as dangerous as everyone says, then I will be at risk, won't I?'

'Of course there will be others there, our agents. Don't worry, you won't be doing this alone. We'll be looking out for you every moment while you're there.'

'I should hope so.' She sat back in her

seat, shaking her head in astonishment. 'But then how can I recognize him if I have no idea who he is?'

'He says you do know him. When you meet him tomorrow at that cafe, he will greet you as an old acquaintance. He will mention something that only you will understand, something I believe about how you met.'

'And then what?'

'Once you have acknowledged him, whoever he turns out to be, that is as far as you go with this,' he said. 'One of our people will be waiting to take you right away from the café. Or more than one person, most likely. Trust me, we will be taking no chances with your safety. I have made that clear to everyone. That was my condition.'

She thought about all that for a moment. 'When you say they will take me right away . . . ?'

'I mean exactly that.' He said emphatically. 'We'll have a car waiting, just at the curb. We'll even have the motor running. As soon as you have identified him, you will be whisked to the airport at high speed and you will leave Paris immediately. Back to New York, and safely away from any danger. Where, it is to be hoped, you will forget entirely everything that has happened to you in the interim.'

Fat chance, she thought, but aloud she said, 'And Mr. Kousinov? The missing man?'

'Who will be missing no longer. He will be our prisoner. Or our guest, depending upon how you want to look at it.'

'And all the danger is past.'

'Perhaps not quite all,' he said frankly. 'Not quite for everybody.'

Her eyes flew open wide. 'You?'

'Not me so much, I should not think. But make no mistake, from the moment you identify him, Kousinov will be in danger, grave danger. Those for whom he works will see him being taken away by U.S. and French agents. This will put their political scheme at peril, the original assassination plan. They have no idea we already know of that, so of course they will not want him to talk to us about it. They will try to prevent his telling us about that.'

'They will try to kill him, you mean.'

His eyes fastened on hers. He was a long moment answering.

'That's entirely possible,' he said finally. 'That they will try. It's my job to see that they do not succeed.'

And you will be the one caught in the cross fire, she thought but did not say.

'This Kousinov' she said instead 'do you believe him? He sounds to me like a very slippery character.'

'He is. But, believe him? In what way?'

'Well, this defection, for instance. Do you think it is the real thing? Or is he just up to another of his tricks?'

'Maybe he is. Maybe not. All anyone can really say is we can't afford to not take the chance that he means it.'

'And the assassination plot? That's still on?'

'It is unless he tells us how to foil it. That is his big bargaining chip. He knows all the details of how this is planned. We don't. All we really know is that it is planned. But what the exact arrangements are, only he knows.'

'Do we at least know who they intend to kill?'

He tightened his lips in a grim line. 'We do.'

'But you're not going to tell me?'

'I don't see how it can matter much now if I do or don't,' he said. 'If Kousinov doesn't play along with us, the whole world will know in a few days.'

'And?'

'And, how do you think the world will react if they believe the U. S. had a hand in assassinating General de Gaulle?'

She gasped in astonishment. 'But surely, you must be joking. Their plan is to assassinate General de Gaulle?'

'Do I look as if I am joking?' His expression was bleak.

She stared hard at him across the taxi's rear seat. 'No, of course you don't,' she said. She sank back into the upholstery. 'But still, they are angling for big fish, aren't they? And somehow I have become a part of all this. I am not even sure just how that happened, to be honest. It all started with a simple mix up at the airport, and now here I am on my way to Paris and a meeting with an international criminal.'

'You were no more than the innocent fly stepping into the spider's parlor,' he said.

'And now I seem to be caught in his web.'

'Yes, there you are. And until that meeting tomorrow in Paris, there's no way of extricating you, however much I might wish to. And believe me, I would if I could. But he insisted upon you.'

She knew perfectly well, of course, that she could easily enough extricate herself, if she so chose. She had no obligation to any of them, to any of this. She wondered what he would say or do if she simply walked away from it all. From the flight, from Paris, most especially from that meeting tomorrow with Kousinov which, pretend though she might, did scare her.

But she knew she could not actually do that. Even as she glanced out the taxi's window, and saw that they were arriving at the airport. The time when she might have walked away was past. With every step that she took now, she was more firmly committed.

But when had that been, the moment

146

when she might have walked away? It seemed all along as if she was just taking one simple step, nothing that could not be undone. And then another step, and another, until now she saw that she was, as he had put it, completely ensnared in Kousinov's web of deceit.

But it was not just a question of timing, either. The Professor had asked her if she considered herself patriotic. She had replied that she had never really thought about it. And so she had not. But even without thinking about it, one knew, in one's heart, that where your country was concerned, you did what had to be done. It did not even warrant thinking about it.

'Next stop, Paris,' Richard told her as he handed her out of the taxi.

'Yes. Next stop, Paris,' she echoed him. And one more step into the center of the web, she found herself thinking morosely.

12

The flight was uneventful, if considerably more grand than Cindy, who invariably flew coach, was used to. One thing she could say for Air France, they seemed to have an interminable supply of champagne, and not the cheap stuff either. But of course, this was first class. She found herself wondering, somewhat cattily, what the peasants in coach were drinking.

By the time they were in another taxi, on their way from the airport to the George Cinq hotel in Paris, Cindy was feeling just a slight bit tipsy.

So that might have contributed to her strange experience. As they were racing through the streets of Paris, she happened to glance out the cab's window in time to see someone familiar emerge from the door of one of those small neighborhood hotels, pausing on the steps outside to glance around. Though common sense told her he was too late to see her in the taxi, she nevertheless shrank down in her seat.

But surely her impression was a mistake. That could not have been Alexie Christophorus she had just seen, coming out of the modest little hotel. It was too much of a coincidence to suppose that he was in Paris at the same time as she was. Unless, that is, he was following her. But why should he be? Yes, he had been protecting her, in a manner of speaking, when she was in Athens but that was days ago, and surely his obligation did not extend this far.

Or was that true, that he had been there to protect her? Emily Gardner had said something that had led her to think that. But what exactly had Emily said, and how much of it could be believed anyway? She had said that there would be someone close at hand, keeping an eye on her. And then Alexei Christophorus had stopped at her table and introduced himself at the Grand Bretagne bar.

But he had not actually said he was the protector Emily had promised. Cindy had just made that assumption. All Christophorus had really said was that he was a reporter.

Which, if that were true, could of course explain his being here. It was not impossible that the press might have gotten wind of Kousinov's defection. Good reporters often seemed to pull their tips right out of the ether. Ought she to mention any of this to Richard? And for that matter, what could she tell him? Whatever Emily Gardner had said, or even hinted at, could not be trusted it seemed.

For that matter, after all, she might only have been mistaken in thinking she had seen Christophorus. It was just as likely that this had simply been someone who looked like the Greek and she was, not too surprisingly, spooked by that upcoming meeting. For that matter, she knew perfectly well she was even a bit giddy from all that unaccustomed champagne on the flight.

No, Richard had quite enough on his mind as it was without having to cope with her fantasies. Still, they were passing a street sign and she had the presence of mind to look out the window again: According to a sign they passed they were on the Rue des Freres, and surely they had traveled no more than a block, or maybe two, from the hotel where she thought she had seen Alexei Christophorus. Even if she was mistaken, and surely she must be, it could not hurt any to know where she was. Just in case . . . but, in case of what, she wondered?

'This is Montmartre, isn't it?' she asked aloud.

Richard paused to glance out the taxi's window.

'Yes, it is. Why, did you see something?' Richard asked beside her.

'No,' she said. 'Just one of those faces in a crowd.' And she repeated to herself, Montmartre, Rue des Freres. She had no idea why she had taken the actions she had taken, or why she should think it important to know where she was just now. But things had gotten so confusing, it could be difficult to sort the various threads out. It felt good to know, that was all she could have said.

'That's the thing about Paris, isn't it?' she said.

'Is it?' He gave her a blank look.

151

'I just mean, it is such a crossroads, isn't it? It's like Hollywood and Vine, I suppose, though I've never really been there. I am sure it is the same thing, though. You hear so much about it. I am sure that when you are actually there, you keep thinking you are going to meet someone you know, is what I mean. Because everyone says you do. So you do, sort of, but it is not really them, not who you think you saw. It is just your imagination playing tricks on you, because you think you are supposed to.'

She thought a moment. 'I wonder,' she said, 'if that's all the Professor's missing man was. Just a mistaken face in the crowd?'

'We'll know tomorrow,' he said.

'Yes. Tomorrow.' Somehow that word had never seemed so ominous to her.

They arrived soon after at her hotel. She started to exit the taxi, but he stopped her with a hand on one wrist. 'I'll pick you up for dinner at, say, eight o'clock this evening,' he said.

'Actually,' she said, 'I was thinking I would just have something sent up and eat a quiet dinner in my room. To be honest, my nerves are a bit jumpy. I don't know if I will even have any appetite. I'm sure you can understand that.'

'Your nerves will only get worse, sitting alone in a hotel room,' he said. 'Believe me, I have been there. Anyway, here is how I see it. I am in Paris, which I think of as the most beautiful city in the world. I have a beautiful companion, and an entire evening free to amuse myself as I will. And best of all, someone else is paying for it. The way I look at it, I would be a fool not to take full advantage of the opportunities that have been handed to me. On a platter, as it were.'

She smiled despite herself. 'And speaking as someone on the platter, you would think me a fool, too, not to share the opportunity.'

'Exactly,' he said, returning her smile.

'Well,' she said, 'Call me anything, but not a fool. Eight o'clock it is.'

Thus by such simple means was set in motion the most wonderful evening of her life. Dinner at La Tour D'Argent, the legendary restaurant overlooking Notre Dame. She had pressed duck, the restaurant's famous speciality, and thought it altogether too bloody for her tastes, but she ate it anyway, because ... well, because this was La Tour D'Argent. After dinner, which ended with an ethereal chocolate mousse and some superb cognac, they had coffee at some little bistro hidden away near Montmartre where they were the only patrons.

'It's early evening for Paris,' he said, indicating the otherwise empty room. 'Parisians are late night people.'

'Like the Greeks,' she said, and did not explain that she liked being there alone with him. A crowded room would only have intruded upon the romantic atmosphere.

After that he took her to a modern day dance club on the banks of the Seine and, the perfect finish to the evening, a stroll along the moonlit river, while a bateaux sailed slowly by. She waved happily to the late evening diners they could see on the boat.

It was after midnight when they kissed good night at the door to her hotel, and, floating inside on a cloud of champagne and kisses, she realized she had fallen quite in love.

'Don't be a daffy, my girl,' she told herself in the privacy of her room, 'He is an international agent, in town for the night. He was glad to have a girl's arm on his, but it could just as well have been any other girl's arm.'

Which mitigated in no way the delicious dreams that she savored through what was left of the night.

While, at his separate hotel not so very far away, a hotel somewhat less grand than hers, Richard Cranston was enjoying some romantic dreams of his own.

13

They had arranged for him to pick her up in the lobby of her hotel at noon the following day. She was already downstairs and waiting when he came in from the street almost exactly at twelve.

'Will we have time for lunch?' she asked, hurrying at his side to the big official looking car idling at the curb. An American Cadillac, she noted, black and looking a block long if not longer.

'Much as I would like to, I'm afraid not. He has set the time for one o'clock,' he said, helping her into the rear seat and sliding in beside her.

'One o'clock? Isn't that sort of an odd hour for such diabolic doings?'

'From his point of view, it's a perfect time,' Richard said. 'The office brigade will still be having lunch, while the tourists are either still eating or having a nap in their hotel rooms. The fewer people about, the fewer witnesses to his perfidy. The better for him.'

'This is quite a switch, isn't it?' she said, running her hands over the car seat's plush upholstery.'

'A switch?'

'Last night we were in something smaller, more Spartan.'

'This is a company car. Last night, we were in mine. Or, to be more precise, the Fiat I rented. I couldn't have afforded something like this, if the rental company had had one, which I doubt. Here, I am supposed to give you this.' He took a handgun from his briefcase and held it out to her.

'A gun? But I've never used one in my life. I wouldn't even know how.'

'It's standard procedure. No agent goes into this kind of assignment unarmed.'

'But I am not an agent.'

'True, but you are walking into a dangerous situation. Anyway, I have my orders.'

'But I don't want it.'

'Fair enough. Here, give me your purse.' He took her purse from the seat between them where she had set it, opened it and dropped the gun inside, and clicked the purse shut again. 'There, put it over your shoulder.'

She did so. 'Now,' he said, 'I have followed the instructions I was given and provided you with a gun, and the rest is entirely up to you. If you would prefer you can just forget all about it until it's time to give it back.'

She hefted the purse in her hand. 'It is heavy,' she said. 'It will be hard for me to forget why.' She studied him for a moment. 'But why should I need a gun anyway? You will be with me the whole time, won't you?' she asked.

'Not with you, exactly,' he said reluctantly. But I will be close at hand for the entire operation.

'Where exactly is close at hand?'

'I will be in this car, and at the curb, simply not in front of the café. But it will be parked just around the corner.'

'But I thought . . . '

'This is all per Kousinov's instructions,' Richard said firmly, in a no-more-discussion tone of voice. 'He wants to meet with you one on one, at least initially.'

'You did say there would be agents nearby.'

'And so there will be. They will be no more than a few seconds away. As soon as you have identified him, you are to take this scarf,' he handed her a bit of silk chiffon in bright scarlet, 'from around your neck and wipe your brow with it, as if you were sweating.'

'I almost certainly shall be,' she said.

He laughed, but with no real mirth. He did not like this arrangement one bit, and he had said so to everyone who would listen and a few who had not. 'When you wipe your brow with the scarf, it will be the signal for our waiting men. They will swoop down within mere seconds, to place him under arrest and take him away. Another group will be right behind them, to whisk you out of there. It will all be so swift you will hardly know what happened.

'Trust me, I'll know,' she said grimly.

'My poor darling,' he suddenly said in an entirely different voice. 'I am forgetting this is all so new to you. Believe me, we have done arrangements like this a thousand times or more. We have got it all down to a science.'

'I just keep thinking, what if something should go wrong?'

'Nothing will,' he said, reaching across the wide seat to give her hand a pat. 'I promise you.'

They swerved in traffic and glided smoothly over to the curb, only a few feet from a sidewalk café. It looked like much any other sidewalk café in Paris, except to Cindy's eyes it was utterly grim and forbidding.

She suddenly wished none of this had happened, that she was still back in New York City, following her usual daily routine, never having heard of Athens and an assignment that would take her there.

'Are you all right?' Richard asked.

'I will have to be, won't I?'

'There is still time to call this off, you know. I can't, but you can.'

'No, I don't think I can either. But promise me that you will be close,'

'I give you my word. Just around that corner, there. And that car right in front of us, the gray Citroen, the three men you see standing alongside it are our agents, just waiting for that signal from you. You remember?'

'I'm to wipe my brow with this. Like a demimondaine.' She laughed and waved the bright red scarf flamboyantly in the air between them.

'Exactly,' he said, and, more seriously, 'And this is not a laughing matter. Come with me.'

They got out of the car and approached the gray Citroen and the men he had indicated. The trio seemed to stand to attention as they walked up.

'This is Spangler,' Richard said, indicating a man in a gray topcoat. 'Spangler, Miss Carter. Once I leave, she will be in your hands. And, Miss Carter, do not under any circumstances leave with anyone other than Spangler here, no matter what they might tell you nor how convincing it may seem. Is that clear?'

'Yes. I am to trust myself to Mr. Spangler, no matter what.'

'Correct. He'll come for you as soon as the other business is finished. Now, is everyone clear on how this is coming down?'

'Totally,' Spangler said, giving her a hesitant smile. She managed to smile back despite her nervousness.

'Absolutely,' she said. 'Well, then, I guess it's time for my Mata Hari act.'

'Darling,' Richard said, and when she paused to give him a questioning look, he said, 'The scarf.' He motioned to his throat.

'Oh, of course, how silly, I can't even give them the signal without that.' She paused to collect the scarf and tie it around her throat, stooping down to study the effect in a rear view mirror. 'There. At least it's a vivid color. No one could possibly miss it.'

She gave her hair one last pat and somehow managed a smile for all four of them, looking more confident than she felt. Richard gave her a quick hug and a peck on the cheek. Then he hastily re-entered the black Cadillac and closed the door after himself, disappearing behind the smoke colored glass.

In another moment, the car had glided smoothly away from the curb. She watched it vanish around the nearby corner. Even knowing that he had promised they would be parked just out of sight there, she found herself wishing he would remain where she could see him.

'Mister Spangler,' she said, giving him one last nod. He smiled reassuringly. 'I guess I'm ready. Keep an eye on me, please.'

'We will, I promise,' he said. 'You are not alone.' He indicated the two men standing nearby.

'I'm counting on that,' she said, and turned toward the tables and chairs arranged in a neat little semi-circle just a few feet away.

And where should she sit, she wondered as she approached them? She studied the seating arrangement a moment more. At the moment it seemed as if she were the only customer the café had, although there was one less than a block away at which, she could tell even at this distance, all the tables were occupied.

Or had things been carefully arranged so that she and Kousinov would have this place to themselves? That, she thought, was the more likely explanation. The NATO agents would not have wanted any errant tourists getting in their way at the crucial moment,

Surely, she decided, it would be best if she sat right up front, where anyone could see her the moment he approached. And it would be faster afterward to make her getaway, the only part of this scenario she actually could look forward to.

She had no more than chosen a spot, at the very front, as close to the curb as she could get, and set her purse atop the little zinc table, than a familiar voice said, 'Miss Carter, I am glad to see you. I was afraid you might not be coming. I cannot say I would much blame you if you had not.'

Cathy stared open-mouthed at the woman who walked up just then. 'Miss Gardner?' she said, astonished. 'But no one told me you would be joining me.'

'I am not. Not exactly. I just needed to bring you this.' She set a now familiar overnight bag on the table beside Cathy's purse.

Cathy stared. 'Is that the same case?'

'It is. The very same.'

'And its contents? Are they the same as well?'

'The money? Oh, yes, every penny of it is there. I assure you.'

'But I don't understand. Why do I need that, here, now?'

'Kousinov is a professional. Wherever he goes, he will need money,' Emily Gardner said. 'In any case, he insisted on this. I am only following his instructions.'

But did she not know that within the next few minutes, Kousinov was to be arrested, by French and NATO agents, Cindy wondered? After which he was unlikely to have need of money? Cindy opened her mouth to explain this to her and thought better of it. She had already learned not to trust Emily Gardner any further than she had to. And perhaps it was just as well if Emily did not know everything.

'Yes? You were about to say something?' Emily asked, watching her closely.

'No,' Cindy said, 'Well, only that, I was under the impression that Mr. Kousinov had insisted I be alone.'

'As you shall be. I was instructed simply to leave the money with you, which I have done. As of this moment, I am officially out of the picture.' She started to walk away.

'Wait,' Cindy said.

Emily Gardner stopped a few feet away and looked back over her shoulder. 'Was there something else?'

'You said, you were instructed,' Cindy said. 'But by who?'

'By whom.' Miss Gardner smiled. 'And surely you have learned by this time that the less you know, the better.' She continued on her way without answering Cindy's question.

14

Emily vanished into the doorway of a small shop a few feet along the sidewalk. At almost the same moment, a voice said, at her other shoulder, 'Miss Carter.'

Cindy turned, gasping in astonishment to see Mike Dillon standing there. Hadn't she understood that this was intended to be a private meeting? She was beginning to feel like she was hosting a convention.

'Mike. But, but what are you doing here?' she stammered. 'I thought you were to do those travel pieces on Athens, the ones I was originally assigned. How is it that you are even in Paris?'

'I don't know, exactly,' he said. 'I was promised the scoop of a lifetime, the sort of thing that could guarantee me a job as a real, honest-to-goodness reporter. I broke all kinds of records in getting here. And I am afraid I burned all my bridges behind me. I am no longer with Columbine, though I was promised this opportunity would be well worth my resignation.'

'Promised? But by whom?' she asked.

He waggled a finger at her. 'Now, now, you aren't going to try to cheat me out of another plum assignment, are you? I suspect you already know as much as I do, maybe far more.'

'In which case you would be mistaken,' she said. 'I'm afraid I am very much in the dark at the moment. About nearly everything, it seems.'

'Then maybe we should compare notes,' he said, starting to sit at the table across from her.

'No,' she said abruptly. 'Don't sit down.'

'But why ever not?' he asked, remaining at something of a crouch.

'You just must not,' she said. 'I can't take time now to explain. And In fact, I'm afraid I will have to ask you to leave. Immediately. Please.'

He looked crestfallen at her. 'Then you do know things you won't tell me.'

'Think what you like' she snapped at him, 'Only, please, I beg you, go. Now.' If

Kousinov was nearby, if he saw her engaged, the whole plan might go awry. And, rightly or wrongly, everyone would blame her.

'Okay, okay, I know when I'm not welcome,' Dillon said with a sulky expression. He whirled smartly about and strode off. And none too soon, she thought. She looked across the sidewalk and saw a familiar figure walking toward her table.

'Mister Christophorus,' she cried. Indeed, it was the man she had met at the Grande Bretagne, stopping now right beside her table, so close that his hip actually grazed the table top. 'It is you.'

'Yes, Christophorus, as some know me,' he said, smiling. 'Although I have had many names in my lifetime.'

'Then you are the missing man?'

His expression was blank. 'I do not know what you mean,' he said. 'I am not missing, as you can see. I am standing right next to you.'

'Oh, that was just what Professor Landos tagged you. The missing man.'

He smiled then, and nodded. 'Ah, yes, the good Professor Landos. And that is all he told you about me?'

'Well . . . ' She squinted up her eyes. 'There's a whole dossier on you, as I understand it. Let me think. He said you were a communist, a traitor to the Greek cause. At one time you went by the name of Ares.'

'The war god.' He gave her a patronizing smile. 'But as I already told you, I have had many names throughout my lifetime.'

'Including Kousinov?'

'Including Kousinov. Do you remember our first meeting, Miss Carter?'

'At the Grande Bretagne, in the bar, of course,' she said. 'I was having lunch and you came up and joined me at my table. At the time, I thought . . . '

'So then you have identified me, yes?' he interrupted her. 'And are you not now supposed to give some sort of signal? Perhaps with that scarf? Which, by the way, does not go at all with the rest of your outfit. Which tells me you did not select it. Might it not have come from Mister Cranston?'

'The scarf? Oh, yes. The scarf.' She

took it quickly from around her throat and wiped her brow with it, as she had been instructed.

Richard had certainly been right about the swiftness of what followed. She was still holding the scarf, knotted into a ball and clenched in her fist, when four men hurried up to the table, seeming like water to flow into positions that had Christophorus surrounded.

All four of the newcomers wore beige topcoats. Although the other three were bareheaded, one of them, the man who seemed to be in charge, wore a brown fedora as well, pulled down so that much of his face was shaded from the sun. Shaded, as well, she realized, from watching eyes.

'Mister Kousinov?' the brown fedora asked and, when Christophorus only replied with a rather strange smile of amusement, the man added, 'You will come with us please.' They started away from the table.

'Wait.' Cindy had half risen from her chair.

Surely she was mistaken, that man

171

could not be who he appeared to be. But she could have sworn that the one with the hat was the man she had last seen in the little square outside Professor Landos's apartment. What had the Professor called him? Janus. That was it.

But surely this could not be he. It made no kind of sense. Janus, working for NATO?

'Yes, of course,' the man said, pausing in his progress. He nodded briefly in her direction and came back to the table to snatch up the overnight case sitting there, the case with, if Miss Gardner were to be believed, one hundred thousand dollars in it. 'We mustn't forget this, must we? Thank you for reminding me.'

With that they were gone, hurrying in a little cluster across the sidewalk, with Christophorus in their midst and the man in the brown fedora carrying the overnight case with its small fortune.

And in what seemed the very next instant, there were three other men at the table.

'Miss Carter,' Mister Spangler said, 'Come with us, please, and quickly. I am to see you safely to the airport.'

He too was wearing a topcoat, this one gray, draped like a cloak over his shoulders, and she saw when he moved his arm (deliberately?) that he held a gun in one hand. Clearly, he was taking no chances with her safety.

'No, wait,' Cindy said, standing so abruptly that her metal chair nearly toppled over backwards to land on the sidewalk. No one moved to catch it. All three were focused entirely on her. 'I must see Richard, immediately,' she told Spangler.

'Miss Carter,' Spangler said, looking irritated and obviously prepared to argue the point with her, 'you heard him give me my instructions in no uncertain terms. My orders are to see you safely to the airport, immediately.'

'Yes, yes, I know what your orders are, and mine too, but I tell you, I must see Richard Cranston, at once. He's parked just around that corner, there.' She pointed toward the corner about which his car had earlier disappeared.

She looked past the trio of NATO agents and saw that the other men headed by Janus had already bundled Christophorus into a small dark car sitting at the curb, its engine idling. It seemed no more than seconds before one of them had jumped behind the wheel and the car rushed away from the curb, tires squealing, pedestrians scattering.

'Oh, it's too late,' she cried, 'They're getting away.'

'What's going on here?' a familiar voice demanded, and Cindy looked in that direction to see Richard hurrying toward them. 'Spangler, you were supposed to have her away from here by now and halfway to the airport.'

'Sir,' the man with the gun said, 'The lady refused to come with us. She said she had to see you.'

'It's my fault, Richard, the blame is all mine.' Cindy ran to him. 'Something's wrong. That man, the one who took Christophorus away . . . '

'Kousinov, you mean?'

'Yes, yes, Christophorus, Kousinov, whatever you want to call him. I'm certain that the man in the brown fedora was Kousinov's old right hand man.

Professor Landos called him Janus. I saw him, that day I visited the Professor. He was watching the Professor's apartment. I think it might have been he who planted the bomb that . . . the bomb.'

'Janus, here?' Richard looked astonished.

'You know him, then?' she asked.

'Janus? Yes, I know who he is, of course I do, but . . . are you sure it was Janus? He is supposed to be back in Greece, according to my information.'

'It was him, I'm certain it was him, right here, to collect Kousinov. But we're too late, they've gotten away already.'

Richard's face grew ashen. 'My God, if you're right there will be all hell to pay. Wait here. Stay with her,' he told the three confused looking agents. 'Don't let anything happen to her or I'll have your butts for breakfast.'

He ran for the corner, disappearing around it. It seemed an eternity before he returned, this time only walking swiftly. 'You were right,' he told Cindy. 'It was Janus. This has turned into a debacle. Our agents were diverted. The Russians must have had this planned all along. They have made us look like fools.'

'What's worse, Janus took the overnight case. They've got the money, too,' Cindy said.

'No, that clever they were not,' Richard said, with a rather wan smile. He lifted up the attaché case he carried, for her to see. 'I'm afraid he will find himself with nothing more than a few wads of old newspapers. Greek newspapers, though I doubt he'll appreciate the joke. I take it that means Miss Gardner was here?'

'Briefly, to drop that overnight bag off with me. When she left, she went into the third shop there. No, the fourth, that patisserie. And I have not seen her come out. So far as I know, she is still inside.'

'I doubt it. But go take a look, just to be sure,' he told Spangler.

Spangler was back in fewer than five minutes, carrying a folded sheet of paper. He handed the note to Richard. 'She left this with the shopkeeper for you,' he said.

Richard unfolded the note and scanned it quickly. 'She already knows about the switch with the money,' he said.

176

'She must be in touch with Kousinov, then,' Cindy said. 'Or Janus. He was the one carrying the overnight case.'

'Kousinov would have taken it from him as soon as they were away from here,' Richard said. 'Janus does whatever Kousinov tells him. He's like a well-trained dog.'

'Yes. Emily said he would need the money. Kousinov, I mean. I thought at the time it was a peculiar thing to say. Why would a man expecting to be arrested need a case stuffed full of money?'

Richard looked up from the note he was reading. 'Surely you don't still trust Miss Gardner, do you?'

'No further than I could throw you.'

'I think you are wise.' Richard said with a chuckle. He went back to the note, seeming to reread it again, more slowly this time. 'She is offering me a chance to redeem myself,' he said aloud. 'A meeting. Where we will allegedly swap the money, for the details of the planned assassination.'

'Will you do it?' Cindy asked.

'Probably,' he said. 'Though I very

much doubt she will live up to that promise. She has not kept any of them yet.'

'Then why take her the money?'

'Actually, it is their money, in point of fact. There is no reason for me to keep it, though it probably was not acquired according to the full tenets of the law. In any case, right now it's the consequences of the murder we have to consider. That is our number one priority.' He folded the note and shoved it into the pocket of his coat.

'And suddenly you trust Miss Gardner?' she asked.

'No more than you do. But for the present she is our only link to Kousinov. It would appear I have no choice but to trust her, at least on this.'

'Take Miss Carter to the airport,' he told Spangler. 'With any luck, there's still time to catch her plane, and she . . . '

'No,' Cindy said, interrupting him.

'No?' He looked at her with one eyebrow raised.

'I did not ask to be written into this drama, but you surely can't imagine I am

178

going to leave before the final curtain falls.'

He met her gaze for a moment, but he was the first to drop his eyes.

'Very well, the hotel, then. Spangler, take Miss Carter to the George Cinq,' he said with a sigh, 'Where, by the way,' he told her, 'they make a very good martini in the bar. Spangler can buy you a drink, on the company. And I promise I'll join you before you've finished the first round.'

★   ★   ★

Twice, Emily Gardner had nearly broken from the patisserie in which she was watching the drama at the sidewalk café unfold.

First had come that fool, Mike Dillon, threatening the entire operation. Yes, it was she who had alerted him to what was going to happen, but she had done so supposing that he would cover it like a reporter, which is to say, observing from the sidelines. She had never for a moment imagined that, seeing Cindy Carter sitting alone at her table, he would approach her and strike up a conversation, while Kousinov lingered in the background, afraid to approach until Ms. Carter was alone, as had been agreed upon. Thank Heaven Dillon had gone as quickly as he had come, and as unobtrusively.

Even worse, though, had been that awful moment when Janus, whisking Kousinov away to the waiting car, had momentarily forgotten the overnight case with the money. The money, half of which was to be her fee for helping with the scheme. Cranston had been right about that, at least. Her chief interest in this, as in most things, was Emily Gardner's well-being. Political advantages put nothing on her table; she had learned that long ago, and the hard way.

But if the fool Janus left the money behind . . . well, half of nothing was still nothing. That time, she had gotten as far as the door, meaning to intervene. She had actually lifted a hand to open it, when something the girl said — from here, she could see everything, but hear nothing — reminded him, and he had turned back to snatch the case off the table, before once again rushing off to the car waiting at the curb.

She let her hand fall. At last, everything was going according to plan. Later, she would retrieve her pay for her assistance. For now, she had only to wait the allotted time. Then she could leave as already arranged, by the back door, content that she had done all that was asked of her.

It was nearly time, then, for her departure, when the owner of the shop, necessarily a party to the conspiracy, came up to her wearing a baleful expression.

'Mademoiselle,' he said, 'I have just had a telephone call from Mister Christophorus. I am sorry to inform you that he says there has been an unfortunate, how do the Americans put it, a snag in your plans.'

15

Emily Gardner's note had instructed Richard to bring the money to an address in Montmartre, which had turned out to be a small nondescript hotel there, on the Rue des Freres. He sat in front for a moment, checking that he was at the right address. Having satisfied himself that he had found the right place, he started to park and then thought better of it. If this was indeed the place, there might be agents watching it, agents who knew his car, even a rental. It could be like a red flag. He drove on and parked a block or so away, as a safety precaution, and walked back, the attache case in his hand, the one with the money in it, seemingly weighing a ton.

The front door of the hotel was locked. He hesitated, wondering if he should ring the bell, but before he could do so the door swung open.

'Richard,' Emily Gardner greeted him,

for all the world as if this were just a visit between old friends, 'How nice of you to stop by.'

He followed her inside, noting that she was careful to lock the door behind him. A squat woman in an apron stepped into the vestibule from behind a closed door.

'Yes?' she asked Richard, ignoring Emily. 'Can I help?'

'It is all right, Martha,' Emily said to her, 'Mr. Cranston is here to see me.'

'The master, he say, no visitors,' Martha said sourly, dying her hands on her apron.

'I am sure he did not mean my old friend, Mr. Cranston,' Emily said sweetly. 'Thank you, Martha, I will take care of everything.'

'The master, he say . . . '

'It is all right, Martha,' Emily said, more firmly. 'I said I would take care of this. You may leave us.'

Martha looked as if she were inclined to argue the point. Then, she said, 'I will be in the kitchen.' With a shrug of her shoulders and a toss of her head, she went out, slamming a door hard behind herself.

'Servants,' Emily said, glowering after her. Then, with a smile, she turned back to Richard. 'But we must not let her spoil our visit, Richard.'

'This is hardly a visit,' he said. 'It's not a social call.'

Her smile faded and she was as quickly all business. 'No, of course you are right, it is not. You have brought the money?'

He held the case up. 'It's all here. But I believe I was to get something in return.'

The door behind her, the one through which Martha had vanished, opened. 'I am afraid Miss Gardner may have promised more than she can deliver,' Alexei Christophorus said. 'That is the money? I will take that, if I may.' He held a gun in his left hand. With his right he reached out for the case.

Richard held on to it. 'I was promised something in return,' he said. 'I expect to be paid.'

'With your life, perhaps,' Christophorus said, snatching the case from his hand, 'If you are lucky. If not . . . well, things do happen. Sometimes unfortunate things.'

'I was to get the money,' Emily said.

'Half of it. In payment for my services. You promised me half the money if I cooperated with you.'

Christophorus gave her an oily smile. 'I am afraid, Miss Gardner, like many of your gender, you have the unfortunate habit of hearing what you want to hear. What I promised was that you would be taken care of. And indeed you shall be. I assure you. I fully expect that a hero's welcome awaits you back in Mother Russia.'

'Russia?' She looked appropriately perplexed. 'But I have no intention of traveling to Russia. Nor should you, I should not think. At this very moment, half the agents in Europe are looking . . . '

'Half the agents in Europe are looking for me just now,' Christophorus finished for her. 'But look as they will, they shall not find me.'

'Can you be so sure of that?' Richard asked.

"I am sure,' Christophorus said.

'Your escape has already been arranged, is what you are saying,' Richard said.

'It has indeed. There is a Russian tanker, waiting in Le Havre to sail late tonight, and a car outside waiting to whisk me there. By mid-morning, we should be free of the English Channel. But, I do hope you understand, Miss Gardner, I am nothing if not grateful. It would be folly for you to remain here when I am gone. Those same agents that you mentioned might very well find you here instead.'

'Especially if they are told where to find me,' she said drily. 'Perhaps by an anonymous phone call.'

'Yes, especially then,' he agreed.

'And what about me?' Richard asked. 'Is a hero's welcome awaiting me in Russia as well?'

Christophorus looked at him with his face expressionless, and only nodded. 'Perhaps. It could happen that way. The Russian leaders are often quite generous where they have reason to be.'

'They would be generous if, say, I cooperated with you, you mean?' Cranston said with a sneer. 'Forget it, I cannot be so easily bought with false promises. And I am not a traitor.'

'No, no I expect you are not,'

Christophorus agreed. 'But we shall see. Sometimes people change their minds.'

'When they are tortured, you mean?'

'Torture? Tut, what an unpleasant word. And one I would not use regarding a guest, which most definitely you must be considered. But for the moment, you will come with me, please.'

'Come with you where?' Richard asked.

'Ah, you do not trust me,' Christophorus said. 'I cannot tell you how sad that makes me. But you must come with me, nonetheless.'

'You still have not said where we are going.'

'There is a room in the attic. Not the most luxurious quarters, but tolerable, as I can attest, having spent some days there myself. You will be reasonably comfortable there while we make arrangements. Later, perhaps . . . well, time will tell. Come, take the stairs there, behind you. I am afraid the lift is not working. 'Janus,' he called over his shoulder.

Janus appeared, gun in hand as well. 'Look after Miss Gardner,' Christophorus instructed him. 'She seems to be less than enthusiastic about our ocean voyage.'

'Ja,' Janus said simply, and gave Emily a malicious leer.

In a moment, Christophorus and Richard Cranston had started up the twisting stairs, Richard leading, Christophorus behind him with the gun held level at Richard's back. They reached a landing and turned, disappearing from view.

★ ★ ★

Richard had been right, Cindy thought. The bartender at the George Cinq's bar did indeed make an excellent martini. Richard had promised Cindy however that he would join her at the hotel's bar by the time she had finished a martini, but he was late. She had all but finished her drink and still he had not made an appearance. Cindy ran her finger through the dregs at the bottom of her glass, not wanting the drink to end, not wanting Richard to be late.

The bartender, plunging glasses into a sink full of soapy water, saw the gesture and shot her a questioning glance.

'Another martini, Miss?' he asked.

She shook her head. 'Not just yet,' she replied and pretended to have another sip from her empty cocktail glass. 'I'm waiting for someone.'

'It looks like he's not coming,' Spangler said in a whisper from the stool beside her, finishing his own bourbon and putting the glass down on the bar with a noisy thunk. It was the first he had spoken to her since sliding onto the stool. Anyone might have supposed they were unknown to one another. 'I'll have another,' he told the bartender.

'What do you suppose might have happened to him?' Cindy asked Spangler directly. There was no point to continuing the subterfuge, it seemed to her. Anyway, bartenders were used to people playing games. She would have been very surprised if this one did not already know that she and Spangler were together, whatever their pretense.

'It's hard to say.' Spangler gave her an apologetic look. 'He might have walked into a trap. That Gardner dame, she's a real piece of work, if you ask me. It wouldn't surprise me in the least if she had arranged a set up for him.'

'And suppose that she has. What exactly can you and I do about it?'

He sighed with regret. 'Not much, so far as I can see. We don't even know where she was meeting him.'

'Since he was told to bring the money, she is probably with Kousinov,' Cindy said.

'That's true, but nobody has any clue where Kousinov is either.'

But I do, she suddenly thought. Or did she? That little hotel in Montmartre they had passed on the way in from the airport the day before. She was sure now that she had seen Christophorus, aka Kousinov, come out of it as they drove by.

Which, of course, did not necessarily mean he was there now, or that Richard was there with him. Still, if there was any possibility . . . it was a slim chance, but the only one they had, to her way of thinking. And surely, in the limited time he'd had, Christophorus could not have arranged for two hideaways in Paris.

'Did you think of something?' Spangler

asked. 'You suddenly had that look.'

'That look?'

'The 'aha look' I call it. When an idea pops into someone's head.'

She shook her head. 'Nothing of any importance,' she said. 'No aha moment.'

If she mentioned that hotel to Spangler, she thought, he would almost certainly mount the cavalry. If she read him correctly, he was the cavalry type, the sort who would immediately ride to the rescue. And, in doing so, quite possible get hostages killed. Get Richard killed, perhaps, if he was a hostage there. And if Richard were there, and seeing that he had not shown up here as promised, then that almost certainly meant he was a prisoner.

On the other hand, one woman, acting alone, might be able to get inside the place, at least to find out if Richard was there. It was the last thing, surely, that Kousinov would be expecting. And he would feel certain he had nothing to fear from her. A mere woman. Suddenly the weight of the gun in her purse felt very comforting to her. She had never fired a gun in her life but she thought most emphatically, if she had to, she would know how.

'I'm going to the powder room,' she told Spangler. 'Wait here, please. And order me another martini.'

Her shoulder bag had been hanging on the post of her chair. She took it down and went all the way through the lobby without pausing at the restrooms, exited through the doors that led onto the Champs Elysée. As she had expected, she found a row of taxis waiting at the curb outside. She slipped the doorman a tip and he opened the door for her of the first cab in the line.

'Rue des Frere,' she told the driver. 'In Montmartre. Just drive the street, but slowly, please. I'm looking for a hotel, and I don't know the name of it, but I'll recognize it when I see it.'

★   ★   ★

Amazingly she did recognize the hotel when she saw it. Or, at least, she thought she did. She told the driver to stop at the curb and sat for a long moment staring at the façade of the little hotel.

Yes, this was it, she told herself, this was the hotel. She was sure now that she had seen Alexei Christophorus come out the front door of this place just as they drove by the day before.

She reached for the door handle, to exit the cab. It was time to see if her suspicions were right. She could only hope so. Because if Richard was not here, if he were a prisoner somewhere else, she had no hope of finding him. In which case, he was almost certainly a dead man.

★　★　★

'Miss Carter.' Emily Gardner looked appropriately surprised when she opened the door to Cindy's knock. 'I did not expect to see you here.'

'I'm looking for Richard Cranston,' Cindy said, and did not miss the quick little glance Emily threw in the direction of the stairs.

'And what makes you think he is here?' Emily asked.

'His car is outside.' That was a bold

faced lie; Cindy had not seen his car, but she thought it a good guess. Richard would hardly have come here on the Metro. Not when he had a rental car to drive. Emily only shrugged. 'It's a busy commercial street. He could have parked and gone any number of places along it. If it is even his car. He rented a little Fiat sedan, did he not?'

She laughed when Cindy looked surprised. 'But, did you not know. We have been watching the two of you since you arrived in Paris.'

She did not add, but thought, and that is because I saw from Richard's behavior in Athens that he had developed a crush on you. It had been her suggestion that the two of them be watched from the time they arrived. She had to argue the point with the Russians, an argument she had won. She had thought the information would come in handy, and it had. Knowledge was power. She was one of the few who even knew that Janus's real name was Jasper. Probably not even Kousinov knew that. Janus himself may have all but forgotten it, but she knew.

One day, she did not yet know how, that knowledge too would prove useful.

'Besides,' she said, 'That little Fiat he rented is a fairly common model. There must be hundreds of them in Paris, maybe even thousands. What is the license plate number?'

'I . . . ' Cindy had to admit she was stumped on that one. 'I don't know the number,' she admitted lamely.

Emily's expression was triumphant. 'Just as I thought,' she said. 'Most likely it was not even his rental car that you saw.'

'I . . . ' But whatever Cindy had meant to say, it was interrupted by the sudden ringing of the bell at the front door.

'What on earth?' Emily said. She moved as if to answer it, but Martha, appearing from the room behind her, was quicker.

'I will see who it is,' she said, and sailed triumphantly past Emily, in the direction of the locked door. She was back in a moment, looking dour. 'It is a reporter, a Mr. Dillon. He says you are expecting him,' she told Emily in a suspicious tone of voice.

Emily was surprised by the news. 'Mike

Dillon? How extraordinary. But let him in, please.'

'The master said . . . ' Martha started to object.

'Oh, bother what he said. And he may be your master, but he is not mine.' Emily swept by her and, going to the front door, turned the lock and flung the door open. 'Mike Dillon,' she cried, 'what are you doing here?'

'Looking for that scoop you promised me,' he said drily, stepping into the foyer. He saw Cindy and was duly surprised. 'Cindy. Miss Carter. I confess I was not expecting to see you here. 'Hello, and you are . . . ?' This to Martha, who had returned from the room beyond accompanied by Janus, who had one hand thrust into the pocket of his jacket.

'Oh, that is only Martha,' Emily said. 'She is the maid.'

'I am proprietress here,' Martha said defensively.

'And you are?' Mike addressed Janus, his eyes dropping to the hand in the pocket.

'An old friend,' Janus said. 'Of the

family.' He seemed to think that funny, and laughed at his own humor.

'Ah.' Mike nodded his head as if he understood, and turned his attention to Cindy instead. 'I hope you are not trying to swindle me out of another important story, Miss Carter.'

'I'm just looking for someone,' she said, glancing toward the stairs. She would have tried going up them, but Janus had positioned himself between her and the stairs. She did not fancy he was likely to let her go past unhindered. If Richard was here, however, and she was more and more inclined to think he was, she was convinced he was somewhere up those stairs.

'Miss Gardner, you promised me a story,' Mike said, turned his attention to Emily. 'A very big scoop, as you described it.'

'I am afraid it might have to wait,' Emily said. 'Maybe even until we get to Russia. Now, there is a story for you.'

'Russia? But I'm not planning on going to Russia,' Mike said, his mouth falling open.

'I am afraid we may not have much

choice in the matter,' Emily said. 'If Kousinov says we go, I am afraid that is what we must do.'

'Kousinov? You mean the Russian spy?' Mike paled. 'What have you gotten me into, Emily?' he asked in an accusing voice.

'You wanted to join the big leagues,' she said, and shrugged. 'When you take on the big time players, the rules of the game change.'

'Except I don't have to play if I choose not to.' Mike took a defensive stance.

'You will do as Kousinov says,' Janus said. 'You are an American fool.'

'That I may be,' Mike declared, 'But, yes, you are right about one thing, certainly, I am indeed an American, an American citizen, and you can't make me go anywhere, Russia least of all. I'm out of here. Miss Carter, do you want to come with me?'

'No,' she said hesitantly, 'I have not yet found what I came here for.'

'Emily?' Mike turned to her. She gave her head a warning shake, trying to tell him that he was playing with fire, but it did not even penetrate his indignation.

'No?' he answered his own question. 'Then I'll go by myself,' he declared angrily.

He had actually reached the door and had one hand on the doorknob, when Janus shot him, in the back. Mike gave one labored grunt and sank to the floor.

'You've killed him,' Cindy cried. She would have run to him, but Janus waved the gun at her, signaling her back. 'Stay where you are,' he said menacingly. 'And shut up.'

He turned the gun on Emily. 'As for you, go into the library,' he ordered her.

'I want to leave,' Emily said.

'So did he,' Janus said with a bark of a laugh, 'And you see how far he got. Into the library, I say. Martha, you stay here and watch that door. See that she does not come out of that room again until we are ready to leave for Le Havre.'

'I will see to it,' Martha said, smiling. She motioned for Emily to go into the next room, and when she had, Martha closed the door and taking a key from the pocket of her apron, she locked it.

'And as for you,' Janus said, gesturing toward Cindy, 'you can come with me.'

He took her arm and marched her toward the stairs. They had barely reached the foot of them, however, before Kousinov appeared on the landing above, descending toward them.

'Ah, Miss Carter,' he greeted her with a smile. 'What a pleasant surprise. I should have known I would see you again. What brings you to our little hotel?'

'I'm looking for Mr. Cranston,' she said. 'I have reason to believe he is here.'

'Indeed he is, Kousinov said. 'I confess that you have found him. Come with me and I will show you.' To Janus, he said, 'I will see to her. You keep an eye on things here. See that no one leaves. And get rid of that.'

He pointed to the body by the door.

16

Alone in the library, Emily wrung her hands together. She had heard the door locked after her. She was a prisoner here, as surely as Mr. Cranston was.

There was no denying it, she had put herself in a dangerous place. She had always known the risks she was taking. She had thought them worth it for the prize that had seemed only a short while before to be within her grasp. Now, there was no money for her, and unless she could think of some way of escaping, she might well find herself on a slow boat to Russia.

But how was she to make an escape? That was the question. Both Kousinov and Janus had guns, while she had nothing but her wits. Unless she used them, and very quickly, she would be on her way to Russia, and regardless of anything Kousinov might promise, she was unlikely ever to return from there.

She knew better than most how meaning-less promises could be. She certainly should have known better than to trust in his. What good would money do her, even if, as seemed now unlikely, she actually got it, if she found herself a prisoner in some Russian gulag?

She had given Mike Dillon this address, thinking that there might be safety in numbers, sure that nothing would be done in front of witnesses, and that hope too had proven unfounded. Janus had shot him without so much as the blink of an eye, and without any concern for witnesses.

And she had always just supposed that somehow Richard Cranston might be the one to come to her rescue, but now he was Kousinov's prisoner as surely as she herself was, and probably soon he would be as dead as Mike Dillon. So, what possible chance was left to her? How was she to extricate herself from the pit into which she had fallen?

Think, Emily, think, she exhorted herself. There must be something you can do. She had always lived by her wits. They surely would not fail her now.

She went to the window and yanked the curtains open, but though the window opened onto the street outside, The Rue des Freres, it was barred. As, she reminded herself, all the hotel's windows were. She had been glad to see that when she had first arrived here. It meant no prisoners were likely to escape. She had little suspected then that in time she too would be one of those prisoners.

She took hold of the metal bars at the window and tugged furiously at them, but they moved not at all. They were too solidly imbedded.

What then? She crossed back to the door, and tried it, but it was locked. Outside, Martha heard her, and yelled, through the door, 'You must stay there. I will say when you may come out.'

Her back to the door, Emily looked frantically about the room, her eyes searching desperately for anything that she might use as a weapon, but she saw nothing that offered her any hope. She looked up at the ceiling, where an old fashioned light fixture glowed brightly, and an idea began to form in her mind.

Yes, the lights. That was a possibility. She had not been thinking clearly. She had been too frightened. Richard Cranston was a NATO agent. Surely he would not have come here alone. Those people did things in groups. In pairs, at least. If he had come inside, there might well be someone else outside, as a back-up. Perhaps even several other agents, but almost certainly at least one.

She hurried across the room, to the light switch by the door and flicked it on and off: three quick bursts of light, and three longer ones. It was a slim chance. First, it depended upon someone's being outside, ideally another NATO agent, or better yet, several of them. And then it would be essential for that someone to know the international distress signal, S.O.S., in Morse code. She knew it, of course. Years ago, her comrades in the resistance movement had laughed at her for learning Morse code. Now, it might very well save her life.

Yes, it was a slim chance, certainly, but the only hope she had of getting out of here without either being killed, or kidnapped to Russia, from which she would almost certainly never return.

She had no illusions about that. If Kousinov did not kill her here, the Russians would certainly kill her or make her a prisoner there. She was a Greek. At one time, she had been associated with the underground. The Russians had long memories. They were like the proverbial elephant. They never forgot.

Again, she flicked the electrical switch: three short bursts of light, and three long ones.

★　★　★

Erwin Spangler had always been a follower, not a leader.

He had been sure earlier that Cindy Carter knew something she was not telling him. The planting of a homing device in her shoulder bag while they were seated at that bar was perhaps the only time in his entire career that he had taken an initiative on his own. It had been easy enough to do. While she had nursed that martini, her bag had hung over the back of her chair, mere inches away from his own. She had not seen him carefully open it and place the device inside.

That, as it happened, had led him here, following her and now sitting at the curb outside that Montmartre hotel. And here his initiative had run dry. He had no idea what to do next, though he was painfully aware that the other two agents with him, sitting patiently in the back seat of the car, were waiting for him to take some sort of lead.

But, to do what?

If, as he suspected, Kousinov was inside, the obvious action would be for them to go in and try to take him prisoner. But there were only three of them in the car, and there was no telling how many men Kousinov might have inside.

The answer to that dilemma was obvious: he needed reinforcements. But he could not summon any without leaving here, and to do so might very well give Kousinov the opportunity to escape. He did not lack for courage, but the fact was, he would look a perfect fool if he were to summon an army of agents to storm that hotel, only to find nobody there.

He scooted about nervously in the car seat.

It was at that moment he heard the shot from inside. But who had been shot, and by whom? The girl? Cranston? That reporter he had seen let inside a few minutes earlier?

He was sitting in a stew of indecision when the lights at the window just to the left of the entry door began to flash. Three short bursts of light, then three longer ones. A long moment of darkness, and then the same sequence was repeated, ruling out any possibility of coincidence. Someone inside was signaling deliberately. Maybe Cranston, maybe the girl, but someone was trying to send a message.

S.O.S. Yes, there it was again, a plea for help.

Meaning, there was no time left to try to summon reinforcements. Whatever was to be done, it was up to him to do it, and it had to be done now.

He swore under his breath. Like it or not, the decision had to be his to make.

And, really, he knew perfectly well, there was only one viable decision. A prevaricating fool he might be, but he could summon the courage when he needed it.

He turned his head and looked at the two men in the back seat. 'Saddle up, boys,' he said. 'It looks like we're riding to the rescue.'

17

Alone in the attic room where Kousinov had taken him, Richard Cranston stared in despair at the locked door. He had already checked the windows and found them, as he had suspected, barred.

What a fool he had been. He had botched everything. He should have known better from the very beginning than to trust Emily Gardner, on anything. He had always known, even back in Athens, that the woman was a snake who would sell her own mother if there was profit in it for herself.

Now Kousinov had both the money and the details of the assassination plot and his side had nothing. And he himself was almost sure to be killed before Kousinov left. In fact, he knew perfectly well that he would be lucky simply to be killed. If Kousinov thought for a single moment that there was any information to be had from him, he could almost certainly look forward to being tortured.

Or, information be damned, Kousinov was a sadistic killer, the sort who took pleasure in killing for killing's sake. And torture, too. He might very well choose to torture his prisoner even if there was no point in it, beyond the pleasure of merely inflicting pain.

Even worse, Cindy Carter was probably also in Kousinov's sights. No doubt she had been from the beginning. At the moment, Spangler was with her, so far as he knew, and Spangler was a good man — certainly a brave one — but also not the brightest agent in NATO's employ. He was most definitely no match for the wily Kousinov.

Which almost unquestionably meant Cindy was a target for Kousinov's schemes. She might already, in fact, be in the man's clutches. And there was nothing he could do to protect or save her.

He went to the window again and tried tugging at the iron bars, but they did not budge. The plaster was flaking around them, though. If he could find some kind of tool, he might be able to dig one or two of the bars out.

A quick search of the room, however, turned up nothing that looked suitable for digging out plaster. In the big old wooden armoire, he found a couple of wire hangers. He carried them back to the window and tried using the end of one to dig at the plaster. After ten minutes or so of serious work, he had made no more than a tiny rivulet in the stone. If he had a year or two, maybe it would work, but he seriously doubted that he would have that much time.

He tossed the hangers aside in exasperation, and started pacing the room again, but a noise at the door brought him to a halt.

Yes, someone was there. He heard muffled voices from outside, and a moment later, a key grated in the lock.

18

Alexie Christophorus took Cindy up three flights of stairs, and along a dusty hallway (Kousinov, she had to remind herself, he was Alexie Kousinov, not Alexie Christophorus).

'Where are you taking me?' she demanded. 'I want to see Richard.'

'And I promised you that you would.' He stopped outside a thick wooden door and, taking a large ring of keys from his pocket, searched through them. He found the one he was looking for and inserted it in the lock.

'You insisted you wanted to see Mr. Cranston. So then, here he is.' He swung the door open. 'Good afternoon, Richard, I have brought you a visitor.'

Richard was standing just inside the door. He and Cindy gaped at one another for a frozen moment in amazement and confusion.

Kousinov laughed cruelly to see them

frozen in astonishment. He put a hand in the middle of Cindy's back and gave her a hard shove into the room, so that she lost her balance and nearly toppled to the floor. Luckily, Richard was there. He caught her in his arms. As she fell against him, she heard the door slam behind her and the key turn once again in the lock.

'Oh, no, he's locked us in,' She cried.

'Never mind about that. The important thing is, are you all right?' Richard asked, holding her at arm's length to look at her.

'Me? I'm fine. It was you I was worrying about,' she said.

'And you came here to rescue me?' Despite their predicament, he could not quite stop a chuckle of amusement.

'Don't laugh,' she told him sternly. 'There are advantages to being a mere woman. People like him don't take us women as seriously as they do other men.'

He held her close and smiled down at her. 'And he should have done, I suppose?'

'Well, he certainly should have thought to check my purse,' she said. She wriggled the purse off her shoulder. 'Do you remember what you put in it earlier?'

He gaped at her in astonishment. 'You don't mean that gun is still there, surely?'

'It must be. I have not taken it out, I can promise you that, and apparently it never crossed his mind to check it. A woman's purse is such a common thing, people almost do not even see it at times. Didn't Poe write something about that, hiding things in plain sight? But why don't you look for yourself and see?'

He did, and brought out the gun he had given her, holding it in two fingers. 'There's something else in here,' he said, 'that you may not be aware of.' He switched the gun to his left hand and brought out a small electronic box in his right.

'A doo-dad of some sort, I would say, but I assure you, it's nothing I put there,' she said. 'So, what is it?'

'Not a doo-dad at all. Actually it's what in my business we call a homing device,' he told her.

'Which does what, exactly?' she asked, though she thought she could probably guess.

'It gives off a signal, which the person who planted it can pick up to see where someone is going. Unless I'm very much mistaken, I think you were followed here.'

'By whom? Spangler? It's true, we were at the hotel bar together and — oh.' She raised a hand to her face.

'I would say you are right, it was almost certainly Spangler,' he said.

'Yes, and that's when he must have put it in my purse, when we were sitting at the bar. Do you think . . . ?' At that precise moment there was a small explosion from below, and shots rang out.

'Unless I miss my guess,' Richard said, 'the cavalry has just arrived. Here, get behind this, just in case.' He dragged the heavy armoire (the nearest thing the room had to a barricade but he was guessing that old, thick wood would stop a bullet) against one wall, making a small alcove of it and the neighboring wall.

'But I have no intention of cowering in a corner like a frightened goose,' she said.

'You're mixing your animals up, it's rabbits who are frightened. And no arguments, damn it. Things might get a little hairy in a minute or two. I would rather see you cower than killed.' He bundled her, none too gently, into the alcove he had created, not noticing that the armoire's mirrored door had swung slightly open as he did so.

He took a moment to check the gun, a handy little .32 caliber, clicking off the safety latch and checking the clip to assure himself that it was still loaded. It was.

If Kousinov came back, he was ready for him. And if he did not return, well, locks could always be shot out.

Things, which had seemed so bleak only a minute or two earlier, were suddenly very much looking up. Thanks to Cindy Carter.

Was it any wonder, he thought, that he loved the woman?

★   ★   ★

Kousinov was descending the stairs. He had made it almost to the ground floor, when the lock on the front door exploded and the door burst open. Three men dashed inside in the explosion's wake. Hearing the ruckus, Janus ran out of the bar where he had taken refuge, gun in his hand, but he had taken no more than a few steps into the foyer before one of the three intruders, the one in the lead, shot him. Janus dropped his gun and fell to the floor.

Kousinov had raised his own weapon, meaning to fire at the newcomers, but seeing Janus fall and realizing that he was sorely outnumbered, he turned instead and ran back up the stairs. The steps were solid, no creaks or groans to give him away, and he was in slippers, so his flight was soundless. None of the people below saw or heard him. No one even knew he had been there. He was still what that old fool of a professor had called him: the missing man.

At the top of the stairs, however, panting from the unaccustomed exertion (at one time, it would have counted for nothing), he paused to assess his situation. This morning, there had been three additional agents with him, but he had dismissed them earlier in the day.

The espionage service of the Soviet Union being what it was, however, he doubted that they had actually gone away when he told them to go. More than likely, they were still somewhere close at hand, perhaps in a car parked across the Rue des Freres, keeping an eye on him just for good measure. Just in case, say, he truly had decided to defect to the West, and everything since that meeting at the sidewalk cafe had only been an elaborate charade, intended to throw his fellow agents off the scent.

It was exactly what he would have done in the same situation: waited and watched, to see what developed. Of course, giving himself all credit, he had not survived as long as he had in the spy business by being a fool.

Which meant if they really were still around, he could count on them now to do one of two things: seeing this hotel raided by a trio of agents — probably, he surmised, agents from NATO, since that was whom Richard Cranston worked for and presumably these men had followed him here — the Russians would either stage a raid of their own, and a shoot-out would follow, with the outcome as yet unpredictable.

Or (and he considered this a far more

likely possibility, since no one, not even a loyal Soviet agent, wanted to die in a gun battle if he could help it, and certainly not when the odds were even, three against three) by now they were hightailing it for Le Havre and the ship waiting there to sweep them out of the country. Without his company, as it happened, but these things could always be explained away. By the time the ship reached Russia, no doubt the three NATO agents just now downstairs would have become, in the reports of the Russian agents, a dozen or more. More, in any case, than they could have been expected to face down. And that, too, was how he would have handled the situation.

With Janus dead, that meant there was no one downstairs who could identify him. Oh, Martha was there, of course, but no one was likely to take her seriously; she could barely converse in English and her French was even worse. Anyone could see in the blink of an eye that Martha was a fool; she could never be more than a pawn in anyone's schemes.

And Emily Gardner was there, too, of

course, but Miss Gardner had always been the consummate opportunist. She could not incriminate him without incriminating herself, and she was smart enough to know that. Miss Gardner would keep her mouth shut, except to find ways to excuse herself.

To that end, she would almost certainly play the part of the mistreated innocent, no doubt with copious tears to underscore her plight. And when her rescuers were no longer paying her close attention, when everyone's head was conveniently turned, why Miss Gardner would simply slip away, and vanish like a wisp of smoke in the night. She was good at doing just that.

And who would care, or why? Who would think the insignificant Miss Gardner could possibly be of any real significance? It was the perfect disguise, her seeming unimportance, which had made it possible for her to survive so long. Which meant, he suddenly realized, perhaps he had underestimated the woman all these years. Something he rarely did.

Well, it was too late to be worrying

about that. Right now he had to think about saving his own skin, and the circumstances of his situation meant, then, that the only two people here who could identify him, who could name him as Alexei Kousinov, who was wanted by espionage agents the world over, were the two locked in the attic room: Richard Cranston and Cindy Carter.

He already knew, had made it his business to discover, that there were other stairs to this hotel. At the far end of this corridor, narrow, and unlit, spiraling stairs could take a man down to a back landing just off the kitchen, where a rear door gave access to an alley beyond.

Those three men who had dashed through the front door would secure the downstairs rooms first, before they searched anywhere else. That meant they would see to the foyer, the library, the dining room and perhaps the bar. Only then would they begin a serious search of the premises.

He knew the drill well. It was what he would do in their place. Agents thought alike in those regards. Always, without exception, you secured your perimeters before branching beyond them. Which meant, by the time they discovered that room in the attic, the two people now in it would be dead, and he would be long on his way.

Yes, with even the slightest luck, he could still get away. Once he was out of the hotel, in that alley behind it, he need only find a car and the gun would help him with that. If necessary, he would simply appropriate one from some passing stranger. Few men were inclined to argue with a gun in their face. And once he was in possession of a car he could be on his way to that tanker, which would surely not yet have sailed, even if the other agents were there. They were expecting him, Alexei Kousinov, not lesser agents. He was an important man, the others were mere fodder. The captain of the ship would wait until the last possible moment before giving up and leaving without him.

That was simply how Russians did things. Nothing was left to chance, ever. But it would be foolish indeed for him to go and leave two witnesses behind. And he was not a foolish man.

He took the ring of keys from his pocket, carefully holding them in one hand to prevent them from jingling and strode noiselessly, on slippered feet, down the hallway, to the attic door.

19

'I have been a prisoner here,' Emily Gardner was just then explaining downstairs to agent Spangler. 'Thank God you came when you did. He was going to kidnap me to Russia. Mostly likely I would never have been heard from again.'

'It was the S.O.S. signal that did it. Good thinking, I would say,' Spangler said.

'It only worked because you recognized the distress signal. You are the true hero here,' she said, looking at him with adoring eyes.

Spangler actually blushed. The role of hero was one to which he was not much accustomed. 'We do what we can,' he said modestly. He turned his attention instead to the two men accompanying him. 'You, Willis, go that way, Berman the other,' he said, pointing. 'Secure our perimeters. We're looking for Cranston, of course, but if you should find the girl instead, bring her to me.'

Emily, of course, could have told him that Cranston and the girl were both upstairs by this time, in that attic room, but she did not. She stepped unobtrusively out of the way, into the early evening shadows by the door, watching Spangler closely.

In another moment, his two companions had gone in opposite directions and Spangler was alone. She saw when he first noticed the stairs, and started toward them, looking thoughtfully upward. Looking away from her.

As quiet as a mouse, she moved to the front door, hanging loosely now from its hinges and, opening it a crack without a sound, slipped through the narrow opening and disappeared into the night.

She waited until she was a block away before she began to run. Her car was not far from here, but not so close, either, as to have drawn attention. Neither Kousinov nor Janus, nor any of their toadies, knew she had it waiting in reserve.

Once she had gotten to the car, she would on her way out of Paris. Never mind her things, they were nothing she could not easily replace. She had learned years earlier the virtue of traveling light.

By tomorrow, she would be back in Greece. No one would ever know or even guess of her part in what had happened here. She was leaving without the money she had anticipated, true, but if it was a choice between her money and her life, well, there was always money to be found, but she had to be alive to find it, did she not? She was no fool.

Yes, there was her car, just across the street. She saw that Cranston's Fiat was parked just behind it. Unlike the hapless Miss Carter, she had taken the precaution of learning its license plate number. How ironic, she thought, that it should be next to her own. Had he known by some instinct that it should not be seen outside that hotel, where it might alert any watchers to his presence? Perhaps he was cleverer than she had thought.

But, she reminded herself, he was now a prisoner back there, probably doomed to die, and she was just getting into her escape car, preparing to leave.

So, he was not as clever as she.

The Rue des Freres was a quiet street, with little traffic at most hours. In the entire time she had been here, Emily had not once had to pause for traffic before stepping into the street. So, engrossed as she was in self-admiration and thinking mostly of the necessity of reaching her car to make good her escape, she dashed into the street without thinking. The approaching car, with three Russian agents in it, was traveling at high speed. Traveling too fast to stop for the woman who had run into the street in front of them. There was not even time to sound the horn before the accident occurred. The driver swerved, not enough to avoid hitting her, but enough that he lost control of the car. It crashed into a lamp pole.

20

At first, Kousinov thought the pair had somehow managed to escape from their attic prison. He opened the door stealthily and saw no one. But that was impossible. There was only one door out of the room, and that door had been locked when he left here earlier. He had just now unlocked it with the key, making hardly any sound at all in the process. So, they must be here.

He looked again, his eyes slowly raking the nearly bare room. There, in the mirror on that armoire's open door: he saw the reflection of the girl, crouching behind the heavy piece of furniture.

Perfect. If he had hold of her, Cranston would quickly give himself up. These Westerners were such chivalrous fools where women were concerned. And gullible; they would believe anything you told them. He would promise them safety, he would swear to let them go. And of course, once they were both in his sights, why then, it would be an easy matter to kill them, the pair of them, after which it was the back stairs and that alley, before anyone downstairs thought to come and investigate the gunshots.

He stepped into the room, meaning to inch his way around to where the girl cowered. But he had taken no more than a handful of steps before a gun fired and Kousinov felt a sharp pain in his abdomen.

A gun? But how had the prisoner come by a gun?

He whirled about, lifting his own gun to shoot back and was hit a second time, this time higher up. He put a hand to the wound. He was bleeding profusely. He tried to lift his weapon, but he was too weak and his hand refused to obey his instructions. He felt the gun slipping from his fingers. It fell to the floor with a loud crash.

A moment later, he followed it.

Richard Cranston stepped from the shadows where he had crouched. 'You can come out now,' he called, and laughed when Cindy came from her hiding place with one of her high heeled shoes in her hand.

'I thought he was coming after me,' she said.

'He was. And he had a gun. Did you really think you could fend him off with that?' He threw back his head and laughed, partly with amusement and partly with relief.

'Ouch,' he cried. Cindy had thrown her shoe with perfect aim, and hit him a glancing blow on the side of his head.

The next moment, however, she had run across the room and thrown herself into his arms, and all danger was forgotten.

Spangler, appearing just at that moment in the open doorway, started to say something and thought better of it.

It didn't matter anyway, he thought, what he might or might not say. Neither of them was likely to answer him, not for the next several minutes.

We do hope that you have enjoyed reading this large print book.

Did you know that all of our titles are available for purchase?

We publish a wide range of high quality large print books including:
Romances, Mysteries, Classics
General Fiction
Non Fiction and Westerns

Special interest titles available in large print are:
The Little Oxford Dictionary
Music Book, Song Book
Hymn Book, Service Book

Also available from us courtesy of Oxford University Press:
Young Readers' Dictionary
(large print edition)
Young Readers' Thesaurus
(large print edition)

For further information or a free brochure, please contact us at:
Ulverscroft Large Print Books Ltd.,
The Green, Bradgate Road, Anstey,
Leicester, LE7 7FU, England.
Tel: (00 44) **0116 236 4325**
Fax: (00 44) **0116 234 0205**

Other titles in the
Linford Mystery Library:

HAUNTED HELEN

V.J. Banis

Mentally scarred by her parents' violent deaths, Helen Sparrow was sent for treatment at a residential psychiatric clinic. Now discharged, she returns to a shadowy old mansion, the scene of both the murders and her repressed, unhappy childhood. But she senses an evil presence in the house: something that follows her along the gloomy halls and whispers just on the edge of her consciousness. Is she insane? Or does some supernatural echo of that terrible night lurk within those walls?

SAY IT WITH BULLETS

Arlette Lees

Two abused and neglected children find sanctuary with a neighboring rancher. Out West, a gold prospector's widow must evade the clutches of a corrupt sheriff. Defying doctor's orders, a wounded cop searches for his missing rebellious sister. After fleeing Hitler's Berlin, a Jewish father and daughter will find unexpected danger in California. A girl's dowdy stepmother is hiding a dangerous secret. And in the gritty underbelly of professional boxing lurks a bloody mystery whose reverberations will echo down several decades.

LORD JAMES HARRINGTON AND THE EASTER MYSTERY

Lynn Florkiewicz

Easter Day — and the vicar's dog digs up a human bone on the Harrington estate. Retracing the dog's walk, Lord James Harrington uncovers a skeleton buried in the woods and identifies a number of expensive items. With the likelihood that the victim could be someone well-to-do, James is concerned that they may be known to him, and puts his sleuthing hat on. His questions take him from Cavendish to Boston, where more surprises await. Will he bring the killer to justice, or is he on a wild goose chase?